*She glanced aro___
going to last a w____
hiding out in the ~~close~~ confines of a
boat with Jude Blackwood?*

A breath shuddered out of her and she rubbed her hands over her face. She'd do whatever she had to, to save her relationship with her sister. So if that meant Cleo was confined to a floating prison for two weeks, then so be it.

"Hey, Goldilocks…"

Cleo shook herself and glanced in the direction of the door. Jude's head came into view.

She lifted a strand of hair. "I'm a brunette."

"And yet just like Goldilocks, you stole into my house."

"I didn't touch your porridge."

"But you plan on sleeping in my bed."

His head immediately disappeared. She gulped and coughed. He hadn't meant in the actual bed *he* slept in. *With him.* He meant his spare bed.

His head appeared in her sight line once more—dark shaggy hair, piercing blue eyes and a scowl. She wanted to tell him to be careful, that the wind might change, but bit the words back. She would be a model passenger, remember?

Dear Reader,

When an image of a heroine leaping aboard a canalboat begging the hero to hide her popped into my mind, I couldn't help wondering who she was and what she was running from. I also saw the way the hero immediately scowled, and I wanted to know the why of that too. And that's how *Secret Fling with the Billionaire* was born.

Former actress Cleo has been trying to leave her scandalous reputation behind. Unfortunately, a series of disastrous high-profile relationships has kept her in the limelight. After the latest disaster, though, she's sworn off men and is determined to make some serious changes in her life.

Recluse Jude is horrified when Cleo literally crashes through the door of his boat. After a recent tragedy, he's been hiding from the world. But sunny Cleo is exactly what Jude needs, and as they work together to keep her hidden from the paparazzi, they find their assumptions about themselves and each other being challenged.

It was so much fun watching this pair engage and retreat, untangling each other's knots and falling in love. I hope you too love Cleo and Jude's journey to happy-ever-after.

Hugs,

*Michelle*

# SECRET FLING WITH THE BILLIONAIRE

## MICHELLE DOUGLAS

**ROMANCE**

# Harlequin®
# ROMANCE

ISBN-13: 978-1-335-21621-2

Secret Fling with the Billionaire

Copyright © 2024 by Michelle Douglas

Harlequin Enterprises ULC
22 Adelaide St. West, 41st Floor
Toronto, Ontario M5H 4E3, Canada
www.Harlequin.com

Printed in U.S.A.

**Michelle Douglas** has been writing for Harlequin since 2007 and believes she has the best job in the world. She lives in a leafy suburb of Newcastle on Australia's east coast with her own romantic hero, a house full of dust and books, and an eclectic collection of '60s and '70s vinyl. She loves to hear from readers and can be contacted via her website, michelle-douglas.com.

### Books by Michelle Douglas

### Harlequin Romance

#### One Summer in Italy

*Unbuttoning the Tuscan Tycoon*
*Cinderella's Secret Fling*

#### One Year to Wed

*Claiming His Billion-Dollar Bride*

*Secret Billionaire on Her Doorstep*
*Billionaire's Road Trip to Forever*
*Cinderella and the Brooding Billionaire*
*Escape with Her Greek Tycoon*
*Wedding Date in Malaysia*
*Reclusive Millionaire's Mistletoe Miracle*
*Waking Up Married to the Billionaire*
*Tempted by Her Greek Island Bodyguard*

Visit the Author Profile page
at Harlequin.com for more titles.

To all of my wonderful readers.
To those who leave reviews, who write to tell me
they love my books, and to those who push my
books into the hands of their family and friends and
order them to read them. From the bottom of
my heart, thank you!

## Praise for
## Michelle Douglas

# CHAPTER ONE

CLEO DUCKED DOWN an alley, her heart pounding and her breath fogging the early-morning January air. How had they tracked her down so quickly?

*Because they knew you'd go to Fairfield House.*

Seeking shelter in the family home in Maida Vale hadn't worked out the way she'd hoped. Her father had woken her precisely thirty-seven minutes after she'd finally fallen asleep to tell her he was tired of her 'attention-seeking behaviour' and that she'd need to find an alternative hiding place.

Apparently an upcoming election was more important than a daughter in need. Especially one as troublesome as her.

*Happy New Year to you too, Dad.* Her eyes stung. She told herself it was from the cold.

Footsteps sounded in the chill air and she flattened herself in the alcove of a doorway, holding her breath when they halted at the top of the alley. They moved on and she instantly sped down the alley on silent feet, grateful to be wearing soft-soled ballet flats. Her feet might be freezing, but at least her footsteps were silent.

The alley led down to the canal path in Little Venice. Pulling the brim of her hat down low, she turned left and prayed it was the right choice. Seizing her phone, she started to dial a number...

Thumbs and feet both faltered. Margot wouldn't come to her aid, not this time. In fact, if Cleo messed this up, her sister might never speak to her again.

A lump the size of Fairfield House lodged in her throat. Why hadn't she controlled her temper, why hadn't she...?

*Enough.*

There'd be time for regrets later. She could whip herself with them then. In the here and now, she needed to focus on not landing on the front pages of the tabloids *again*.

On the path up ahead, another photographer appeared. His back was to her, but he'd turn around any moment. Behind her, she heard the approaching footsteps of the first photographer. Once they reached the path, she'd be cornered. Twisting her hands together, she scoured her surroundings. A wall at least eight feet high towered to her left. She had no hope of scaling it. To her right was the canal. She could swim it. It'd be freezing, but...

*Oh, and pictures of you splashed across the front pages of the dailies swimming in the canal in January will make Margot's day, huh?*

That'd be worse than today's front page!

*Nothing is worse than today's front page.*

Her heart pounded in her ears. She needed an escape hatch if she didn't want to ruin her relationship with her sister forever...

She couldn't go forward.

She couldn't go back the way she'd come.

There was an un-scalable fence one way, the canal the other, with canal boats...

She blinked. An open door on a canal boat named *Camelot* beckoned like a bright star.

Not giving herself time to think, Cleo shot across the path and leapt onto its rear deck, the thin soles of her ballet flats slipping on the slick, dew-laden surface, her arms windmilling wildly and her phone flying from her hand to land in the canal with a soft splash.

*Don't fall in the water! Don't fall in the water!*

Launching herself through the door, she half-slipped down a set of stairs on her backside—not elegant, but certainly efficient.

A lone man glanced up from reading the paper at a dinette. Her picture glared back at her from its front page in silent accusation. Still on her backside, she shuffled to the side behind an arm chair—out of view of anyone who might peer through the door. Lifting a finger, she held it to her lips, then pressed her hands together in a silent plea that he not give her away.

Leaning back, he closed the paper, his gaze

briefly resting on the front page. Glancing back, he gestured for her to remove her sunglasses. She did. She had no control over the way her eyes filled, though. Blinking hard, she gritted her teeth, determined to not let a single stupid tear fall. He looked as if he wanted to swear. She wholly sympathised.

Grinding back what sounded like a muttered curse, he eased out from behind the table with remarkable grace for such a large man—not that he was brawny, just tall and rangy. Something inside her give a soft sigh of appreciation. She slapped it hard.

'Hello?' someone called from outside.

Mr Tall, Dark and Scowling started for the door. Praying he wouldn't pick her up on the way and dump her at the waiting journalist's feet, she seized a beanie resting on the arm chair and held it out to him with an apologetic grimace. It was cold out.

He pulled it on over thick dark hair that looked incredibly soft and…

'Hello?' the journalist called out again.

Blue eyes turned winter-frigid. Swallowing, she handed him her sunglasses before he could turn her to ice. He shoved them on his nose and stomped up the steps.

''Scuse me, mate, have you seen a woman come past?'

Her stomach shrivelled to the size of a small,

hard walnut. *Please don't let him give me away.* She closed her eyes and crossed everything.

'Look, *mate*, only thing I've seen...'

Her eyes flew open at the thick Geordie accent that emerged from her reluctant rescuer's mouth. Had he travelled by canal boat all the way from Newcastle? Was that even possible? If so, he was a long way from home.

She shook herself. What did any of that matter?

*Focus, Cleo.*

'What did you see?'

'A lad scaling that wall there.'

'Could it have been a woman?' The hungry greed in the journalist's voice nauseated her.

'Hard to tell. I called the authorities. Seemed dodgy. And, speaking of dodgy, who the hell are you, and what are you doing chasing some woman? Think it's time I called the authorities again.'

Her tensed muscles released and she rested her forehead on her knees. He wasn't going to blow her cover.

*Thank you. Thank you. Thank you.*

'No, no, I'm just leaving. Not causing any harm. Just an interested bystander.'

Footsteps moved away at a fast clip. Lifting her head, Cleo buried her face in her hands and let out a shaky breath.

Her rescuer closed the door and strode past her to drop the beanie and sunnies onto the table, before filling a kettle and setting it on the hob. Only then did he turn to her, hands on hips, and she had to crane her neck up, up, up to meet his gaze. He gestured to the dinette and she scrambled to her feet, taking a seat.

'You're going to have to wait an hour if you want to give them the slip.'

And then what? They'd be waiting for her at her flat. Her girlfriends' places would all be staked out. 'Thank you for not giving me away.'

He made tea and slid a mug across to her. He didn't ask her how she took it. And he remained standing, leaning against a kitchen bench, one ankle crossed over the other as he blew on his tea.

She took a sip of her tea, welcoming the warmth even if it was strong, black, unsweetened and not what she was used to. The newspaper he'd been reading rested on the table in front of her, a reminder that she'd once again shamed her family. Those days were supposed to be in the past!

Except apparently they weren't. Tears scalded her eyes. She gulped tea and welcomed the burn on her tongue. 'You recognised me.'

He shrugged.

She gestured down at herself. Ditching her usual uniform of jeans and blazer, she'd raided Margot's wardrobe for a pair of sensible black trousers and a caramel-coloured sweater, before piling her hair up beneath a cloche hat. 'I was

hoping this would be enough of a disguise to pass
unnoticed until I'd reached…safety.'

Except nowhere was safe, not from the press.
If the last eight years had taught her anything, it
was that.

'Maybe if you hadn't appeared in the morning paper…'

*If.*

Guilt, regret and remorse all pressed down on
her.

She straightened, registering that his accent
had disappeared. Had he assumed it? What an
excellent idea!

Glancing up, she caught his scowl, and her
shoulders inched towards her ears. 'I'm really
sorry I crashed onto your boat like I did. I was
cornered…desperate.' She fought the urge to rest
her head on her arms. Without meaning to, she
spread mayhem and annoyance wherever she
went.

'Forget it.'

If anything, his scowl deepened, but the unexpected largesse—gruff though it might be—
slipped beneath her guard. She had to blink hard
again. She gulped tea as if it might save her.

'Was he worth it?'

'Who?'

Reaching across, he turned the paper over
and pointed to her photo. The gesture lifted his
rolled-up shirtsleeve to expose a forearm roped

with muscle. A tic started up inside her, but she squashed it flat. She'd learned her lesson, thank you very much—men were *off* the agenda.

Turning the paper to face her, she gave a startled laugh. 'Wow, I really did land a good punch, didn't I?'

'I'd have been proud of it.'

For the briefest of moments one corner of his mouth twitched and she held her breath, but it came to nothing, his face settling back into stern lines.

She sobered too. 'He'd just told me he'd been fooling around with someone *close to me*.'

She drained her tea. He filled it again from the teapot.

'I was as angry with myself as I was with him, though. I'd tried breaking up with him a month ago, but he convinced me not to. Told me he loved me.' Something he'd never done before. 'I was trying to be mature—relationships aren't all rainbows and unicorns, blah blah blah—compromise, put the work in...'

'You sound like a self-help manual.'

Her back straightened. 'I've read them all.' She'd done her homework and had put in the hours. She was on Road Straight and Narrow now. 'For all the good it's done me.' She scowled at her tea. 'Men suck.'

'That one does. Though for the next week it'll probably be through a straw.'

She barked out another laugh, immediately clapping a hand over her mouth. Pulling it away, she shook her head. 'I'm through with all of it. Romance is dead.' The sooner she faced that fact, the better.

'Good for you.'

She eyed him over the rim of her mug. 'Are you laughing at me?'

'Nope.' Pushing away from the kitchen bench, he slid onto the seat he'd been occupying earlier. 'I just agree that romance and relationships aren't the be all and end all. Too many people define their worth through them rather than in more stable things. So when things go belly up...' he shrugged '...they don't have the resources to deal with it.'

She didn't know if he meant the comment to be pointed or not but, given her past romantic mistakes, she'd deserve it if he did. And she'd take it on the chin.

She'd thought that she'd drop out of the public eye when she'd stopped acting two and a half years ago. The men she'd dated since, however, had ensured that had never happened. It meant a lot of people who'd never met her and didn't know her made assumptions about her. And she'd take that on the chin too because, in shielding her from those journalists, this man had saved her butt.

She shivered. She really needed to start making better decisions. Whatever she was searching for, it wasn't to be found in any of the places she'd been looking. She'd thought walking away from acting would change everything. It had changed some things, but not all. Her stomach churned: because *she* was the problem. She kept making the same mistakes. How stupid and self-delusional could one person be? She'd honestly thought Clay had been the one.

*Don't think about that now.*

'In my experience, love is an exercise in deception, disillusion and despair. We'd all be better off without it.'

Whoa. Talk about cynical.

He shrugged at whatever he saw in her face and she shook herself.

*Focus on the practicalities.*

'So…a quick question.'

He tensed.

'An easy one, I think. If I dropped my phone in the canal…?'

'Gone for good.'

She'd guessed as much.

'Need to ring someone?'

She nodded.

Reaching behind him, he stretched one long arm across the kitchen bench to open a drawer and fish out a mobile phone. He set it in front of her.

Picking it up, she dialled Margot's number and left a message. 'My sister,' she explained, her heart giving a sick kick. 'She won't answer a call from an unknown number. But she'll listen to the message and call me back in under sixty seconds.'

She set the phone on the table and started counting back from sixty. The phone rang when she reached forty-four. She glanced at the man and he gestured for her to answer it.

'Cleo?'

'Hi, Margot.'

'You lost your phone?'

'Afraid so. I was—'

'I don't want to hear about it! Just tell me the press don't have it?'

'The press don't have it.'

'That's something, I suppose. Now listen to me, Cleo, and listen hard, because I'm only going to say this once. If you appear in the papers one more time between now and my wedding, I never want to see you again.'

Cleo would've laughed, except she'd never heard her sister sound so serious. And her sister was the *queen* of serious. Her stomach gave a nauseating roll. 'Margot, listen—'

'No, *you* listen! If you ruin this for me, I will never forgive you. I don't want to see you for the next two and a half weeks. The next time I want to clap eyes on you is the morning of the wedding.'

'But…there are the final dress fittings.' Cleo was Margot's bridesmaid—her *only* bridesmaid.

'We'll make do with your last lot of measurements. Just don't go gorging yourself on cheesecake and crisps for the next seventeen days.'

Cleo held the phone away from her ear to stare at it. She pressed it back again. 'What about your hen night?'

'I don't want you there.'

She sucked in a sharp breath.

'In your current form, you'll ruin it.'

Margot's unspoken 'again' sounded in the spaces between them.

'You will lay low for the next two and a half weeks. I don't want to hear a peep about you, I don't want to see any photos of you, I don't want anything you do ruining my wedding. Do you hear me?'

She tried to swallow the lump in her throat. 'Loud and clear. And, Margot, I swear I won't. I'm sorry…'

But Margot had already hung up.

The expression on Cleo's face had Jude wanting to swear.

'No.' She lifted the newspaper and shook it. 'He wasn't worth it.'

All of the vitality drained from those extraordinary olive-green eyes, and his chest squeezed tight, and then tighter still, as if to make sure he couldn't ignore it. He swore and raged silently, and did what he could to pound it into oblivion.

It didn't work. Cleo's downturned lips, the defeated slope of her shoulders, the way tears had sheened her eyes three times now but hadn't been allowed to fall all caught at him, doing its best to drag him out of his self-imposed exile, his hard-nosed detachment.

*Not* going to happen. In an hour, after he'd said farewell to Cleo, he and *Camelot* were heading north. He'd settled his grandmother's estate. There was nothing to keep him here now.

*'Promise me, you'll do one good thing every day.'*

The memory of the promise his grandmother had extracted from him, given reluctantly, plagued him. It'd plagued him for the last week. *Damn it!* If the last nine months had proven anything, it was damsels in distress weren't his forte.

He wrinkled his nose. 'Margot didn't sound best pleased.'

'Understatement much?' She even managed a weak smile.

He stared at it and swallowed.

Slim shoulders lifted. 'It's her wedding in two and a half weeks.'

'She's turned into Bridezilla?'

'No!' Another faint smile appeared. 'Well, maybe a little, but she just wants the day to be perfect.'

As far as he was concerned, anyone who wanted to take the matrimonial plunge needed their head read. 'Perfection is a lot of pressure.'

Cleo blinked and then smiled—really smiled. She had a wide mouth. Her eyes danced, and it was like a sucker punch.

'I don't mean "perfection" in that the sun must shine like it's never shone before, and that there can be no crying babies in the church to break the reverent hush, or that all hell will break loose if the canapés aren't up to scratch—not *that* kind of perfection.'

Okay, she'd lost him.

'Her idea of perfection is that she and Brett will get to stare deep into each other's eyes while they make their vows, that all in attendance will be happy for them and that there's genuine joy at the reception.' She hesitated. 'That all who witness their marriage and celebrate with them will remember the day with fondness—that it'll be a happy memory.'

He ordered his lip not to curl.

'What she doesn't want is for her mess of a sister, who also happens to be her bridesmaid, trailing tabloid photographers in her wake and turning the day into a circus.'

'Are you a mess?'

She held the newspaper beneath her chin. 'I give you Exhibit A.'

*Point taken.* Cleo Milne was a *total* mess. She

might look all sweetness and light, but the media had dubbed her Wild Child for a reason. She'd been an actress on a well-known British sitcom and the kind of woman he avoided like the plague: the kind of woman he'd sworn never to get involved with.

For some reason the front-page spread of Cleo punching her boyfriend—the lead singer of some boy band—reminded him of the look in her eyes when she'd said he'd been cheating on her. His chest drew tight. It didn't matter how famous you were, betrayal hurt.

Reaching across, he plucked the paper from her fingers and threw it face-down on the kitchen bench behind him so she'd stop beating herself up about it. While Cleo might be a mess, her sister wasn't supposed to think that. 'Okay, the timing of that might not have been great, but the berk clearly deserved it.'

*'Do one good thing a day. Promise me.'*

Pulling in a breath, he nodded. 'Right.'

Cleo glanced up expectantly.

'Margot wants you to lie low until the wedding, correct?'

She nodded.

He could help her come up with a plan, and then they could both be on their way. He wouldn't feel like an unsympathetic jerk, she'd have a direction *and* he'd have kept his promise to Gran: win-win.

'Anyway, just wait. This'll all die down in a few days. Once Margot calms down she'll see she's overreacting. She'll want you at the final dress fitting. She'll want you at her hen night.'

Cleo brightened. 'You really think so?'

*What the actual hell...?*

He didn't know Margot from Adam. Resisting the urge to run a finger beneath the collar of his jumper, he soldiered on. 'Until then, you need to avoid the press. Is there somewhere you can go?'

She chewed at her bottom lip. He stared at the way those small teeth made the lip plumper, deepening the colour to a raspberry blush. A hard hunger flared in his gut. Gritting his teeth, he ignored it. 'Your father?'

She flinched and shook her head.

'Other relatives?'

'It's just Dad, Margot and me.'

Why couldn't her father help her out? He bit back the question. Families could be complicated. He knew that. 'Friends?'

'That's where the press will expect me to go. They'll leap out at me from some shady doorway or corner, frightening the bejeebies out of me and snapping a picture of me looking appalled and terrified.'

And Margot would throw another fit.

'Margot deserves better from me,' she whispered.

'Cleo…' It was the first time he'd said her name. It rolled off his tongue like music and mead.

*What the actual hell…?* He was a thriller writer, not a poet! It was all he could do not to curl his lip at himself. *You're not a writer any more.* The unwelcome reminder had him clenching his jaw so hard it started to ache.

'Is everything okay?'

He shook himself. 'How's this for a plan? I'm about to head north. I can drop you on the out-skirts of London somewhere and you can hole up in some country inn or rental for a fortnight.'

Her face brightened. The hard things inside him unclenched a fraction.

*That's two good things, Gran.*

He'd chased the journalist away *and* he was helping Cleo come up with a plan for her imme-diate future.

His lips twisted. *Go him.*

'Or?'

The excited buzz in Cleo's voice had his eyes narrowing. Behind the olive-green of her eyes, her mind was clearly racing. Foreboding gath-ered behind his breast bone.

'Or I could hide out on a conveniently pass-ing narrow boat for a fortnight. I'd pay you,' she rushed on, as if seeing the refusal in his face.

'No.'

She eased back, chewing on her bottom lip

again. His skin drew tight. He resolutely refused to notice that lip.

'I'll be quiet and not make a nuisance of myself, I swear. You'll hardly know I'm here.'

*That* would be impossible. 'No.'

'Why not?'

'The reason I took to the canals in the first place is because I want peace and quiet.'

'You've been travelling around a while?'

'Seven months.'

Her jaw dropped. 'Surely that's enough peace and quiet for anyone?'

He begged to differ.

Her lips pursed—not in any kind of mean or calculating way, but as if she was joining dots he didn't want her joining. Except she didn't know him, so she couldn't be joining dots.

'I know I'm in complete ignorance of your circumstances, but surely a bit of extra income would come in handy?'

He had to stifle an astonished crack of laughter. Yep, she was in complete and utter ignorance. And that was how he wanted it to stay.

She huffed out a sigh, as she read continued refusal on his face. His grandmother wouldn't be proud of him, but he refused to modify his expression and didn't soften it one iota.

'A week, then. Let me stay for a week and I'll pay you twenty-five thousand pounds.'

He had no hope of hiding his shock. He shot

to his feet, whacking his thigh on the edge of the table as he did so. He swore, out loud this time.

She winced and mouthed a silent, 'Ouch.'

He glared his outrage.

She shrugged. 'I'd pay ten times that to save my relationship with my sister.'

*Damn it.*

'If I had it.' Her lips twisted. 'But I don't.'

He folded his arms. 'Do you actually have twenty-five thousand pounds?' He doubted it. She might've been an actress on a successful sitcom for seven years, but Cleo Milne was the kind of person who'd have long since frittered that money away.

She seized his phone and accessed the Internet, eventually turning it towards him to show him a bank account that bore her name. The balance showed just over twenty-five thousand pounds.

'It's my rainy-day fund.' She paused. 'It's the money my mother left me.'

Her *dead* mother. He dragged a hand down his face.

'And at the moment it's not just raining, it's bucketing down so hard that I'm going to drown unless I do something big. The money is all yours if you let me stay.'

He couldn't utter a single damn word.

'I know everyone thinks I'm rolling in cash. And maybe I will be one day if I ever gain access to my funds.'

What was she talking about now?

'But when I started acting I was a minor. My father signed my contracts. When I came of age, he convinced me to have the majority of my acting income put "in trust" for the future.'

Was he withholding it? 'So this…' He gestured to his phone.

'Like I said, it's my rainy-day fund.'

'What do you live off?'

'The fruits of my current labours.'

Which were…? *None of your business.*

'Fine.' He had no intention of taking her money but he had every intention of calling her bluff. 'One week on board the narrow boat *Camelot* at a cost of twenty-five thousand pounds.' He thrust out a hand. 'It's a deal.'

Squealing, she seized it and pumped it up and down. 'Thank you, thank you! You're a lifesaver.' Her entire body vibrated with relief. 'Give me your bank account details and I'll transfer the money now.'

Hell, she wasn't joking! And he'd just agreed…

'What?' she said when he remained silent.

'No.'

Her whole being fell. 'But I don't have anything else to barter with.'

Her eyes sheened with tears again. *Damn it!*

'The only way to ensure I don't get photo-graphed is to not leave this boat.'

He couldn't kick her off *Camelot*, no matter

how much he might want to. He pointed to the phone. 'Check how much it costs to hire a narrow boat for a week.'

She searched the Internet. He made more tea, for himself this time. What the hell was he doing?

His grandmother's voice sounded through him. *'You're doing your one good thing for the day.'*

This had to count for entire week of good deeds! Except he knew Gran wouldn't have seen it like that.

'Okay, here we go.'

She handed him the phone and he handed her another mug of tea before sliding back into his spot at the table to view the information. 'This is for a luxury barge. *Camelot* isn't luxury and it's nowhere near as big.' He fixed her with what he hoped was the steeliest of glares. 'Tell me exactly where you think you're going to sleep.'

'I'm guessing that this—' she tapped the table '—folds down to a bed. Which will do me nicely.' She pointed behind him. 'I can see one corner of your bed from here. I'm not expecting you to give it up for me.'

The narrow boat had a single long corridor, with no internal doors except for the bathroom and toilet.

'There are bunk beds further along.'

She brightened.

'*Not* luxury,' he repeated. The amount showing on her phone was an obscene amount of money.

He wouldn't charge that for a month's worth of accommodation. Not that he had any intention of offering anyone a month's worth of accommodation, no matter how much he might sympathise with their plight or how beguiling he found their eyes. He'd charge her a reasonable amount, though. It'd keep things business-like and professional.

'You haven't factored in that I get my own personal narrow-boat captain, though.'

He raised an eyebrow and tried to look as severe as possible.

She grimaced. 'And I'm going to need a few things…'

He rubbed a hand over his face when he realised what she was getting at—he'd have to be the one to get them for her. 'You're going to make me go into a ladies' underwear department, aren't you?'

He'd know what underwear she was wearing. That would be wrong on too many levels.

She winced. 'Sorry, yes. I'm also going to need a toothbrush, some clothes…and a phone. I'll give you my credit card.'

This woman was too trusting. 'Hasn't it occurred to you that I'm a strange man you don't know from Adam?'

'I know your name is Jude Blackwood.' She picked up some mail on the table to display his personal information.

His hands clenched. She had recognised the name. Did she know…?

She stared back, not a single suspicion lurking in her eyes. He released his breath slowly.

'And I know I can trust you.'

'How?'

'You could've made yourself a pretty penny if you'd made a deal with those journalists and escorted me off your boat. But you didn't.'

She might be a spoiled starlet, but nobody deserved to be hounded like she'd been.

'And I know people. I'm a good judge of character.'

Seizing the newspaper, he slapped a hand on the front page. 'I beg to differ.'

Her eyes dimmed and he felt like an unsympathetic jerk.

'Also, I'm not an idiot.' She thrust out her jaw. 'My sister knows who I'm with and now has your number. She's angry with me, but that doesn't mean she's not going to keep an eye on me.'

Okay, she had him there.

'And, besides the fact that you're all grumpy and growly on the outside, the name of your narrow boat suits you: *Camelot*. I suspect you're more gallant Galahad than misanthrope.'

'You call me that again, and I'll throw you in the canal myself.'

His scowl clearly didn't intimidate her because

she bit her lip, as if trying not to laugh. She gestured to the phone. 'Do we have a deal?'

He knocked two grand off the price.

'Oh, but—'

'And I want your sunglasses.'

He added the last because he knew she wanted to feel as if she was paying a fair price. Those sunglasses might be ugly, but they'd provide an excellent disguise. They'd come in handy when he had to return to the real world.

Cleo froze like a deer in the headlights; like a statue; like a lamb to slaughter.

For a brief moment he thought she might hug the stupid ugly things and burst into tears. Instead, she wordlessly pushed them across the table to him. He couldn't say how he knew, but in that moment he knew she'd rather pay twenty-five thousand pounds and keep her sunglasses. He also knew retracting his demand would offend her deeply. He wanted to swear and swear.

Maybe, despite all appearances to contrary, like Cleo he still knew people too.

# CHAPTER TWO

CLEO REMAINED HIDDEN below while Jude fired *Camelot*'s motor to life, untied the moorings and started along the canal. He seemed ridiculously capable, single-handedly managing the narrow boat with an ease she envied.

And found ridiculously attractive. *Oh no you don't!* She was making some serious changes to her life. Starting today.

*No men. No romance. No making headlines.*

Her days of lurching from one mistake to the next, one disaster to another, had to stop. And all the mistakes that had landed her in the papers over the last three years had involved men. The incident with Clay last night had simply been the last in a long line.

A hard burn stretched through her chest. She should've walked away. She'd planned to walk away. But then he said that awful…*thing*…and her 'sensible and dignified' had fled.

She scrubbed her hands over her face. That *didn't* mean she would fall back into old patterns.

She *hadn't* been drinking. She *hadn't* been seeking distraction or diversion. Not that her father would believe her, or Margot. And she had no one to blame but herself. It was what happened when you let people down too many times—they lost trust in you.

A weight slammed down on her shoulders. The room blurred, but she blinked back the tears. She'd honestly thought she and Clay would go the distance. Sure, she'd had the odd wobble, but she'd thought that if she worked hard enough, if she didn't give up, they could create the same sense of security she'd cherished when her mother had been alive. Security she'd been searching for ever since. But obviously she'd been looking for it in all the wrong places.

A lump stretched her throat into a painful ache. How could she have been so wrong? How could she have deluded herself so completely? Was she really so needy? Was she so incomplete—so *emotionally impoverished*—that she needed a man to make her feel fulfilled?

This had to stop. She didn't want to be *that* person.

*No men. No romance. No making headlines.*

Ewan had dated her to boost his credentials and land a role in drama series. Davide had used her so he could play the victim and gain public sympathy by staging an awful break-up. Austin hadn't cared for anything beyond her looks. He'd been appalled when she'd spent a weekend in her PJs watching old movies and eating popcorn. He'd wanted a trophy to parade in front of his friends.

None of those men had truly known her. None of them had truly cared for her.

And now Clay...

Here was a sobering fact—she was gutted to have been wrong about him, but she wasn't gutted to have lost him. So what on earth had she been doing thinking he was The One?

Pulling in a breath, she let it out slowly.

*No men. No romance. No making headlines.*

So the one thing she *wasn't* going to do now was develop a thing for her unlikely rescuer. Instead, she'd learn to manage her life with the same ease Jude Blackwood managed his narrow boat.

She glanced around. The life he led was pretty...spartan. The money she was paying him would probably be welcome, though it didn't change the fact that he was as happy about her being on his narrow boat as he would be finding dog dirt on his shoe.

But he *had* let her stay. And he hadn't taken her for a ride, as he could've done; he hadn't cleaned out her bank account. So she'd do all she could to be a model passenger. Maybe then she'd be able to convince him to let her stay for longer.

She glanced around again, taking in the dimensions of the boat. Dear God, how was she going to last even a week hiding out in such a tiny space? She'd go mad!

*You'll do whatever you have to, to save your relationship with Margot.*

Her hands clenched. Margot had always deserved better from her. She couldn't wreck her sister's big day. Margot had already forgiven her enough unforgivable things. She couldn't cast even the tiniest of dark clouds over her wedding— that *would* be unforgivable.

If that meant Cleo was to be confined to a floating prison for a week or two, so be it.

'Hey, Goldilocks…'

Cleo glanced in the direction of the door and Jude's voice. 'Are you talking to me?'

'Yep.'

'I'm brunette.'

'And yet, just like Goldilocks, you stole into my house.'

'I didn't touch your porridge or sit in your easy chair.'

'But you plan on sleeping in my bed.'

She spluttered and coughed. He didn't mean in the actual bed *he* slept in *with him*. He meant his spare bed.

His head briefly appeared, all dark shaggy hair, piercing blue eyes and a scowl. She wanted to tell him to be careful, that the wind might change, but bit the words back. *Model passenger, remember?*

Part of her wondered, though, if teasing him

a little might make her the ideal passenger. Jude Blackwood seemed to carry the weight of the world on his shoulders. It'd be nice to lighten his load, if only for a moment.

'Have you had breakfast?'

'Yes,' she lied. She was already enough of a bother.

Those startling eyes narrowed. She tried not to fidget. He pointed to the kitchen bench. 'Make yourself some toast. That's non-negotiable,' he added, when she opened her mouth. 'I'm not having you faint on me from lack of food. You faint, and the entire deal is off.'

She'd hardly faint from skipping breakfast but nodded, model-passenger-style.

'And, while you're eating, make me a list of what you need. Some time this afternoon, I'll stop and get supplies.'

'Is it okay if I have a look around?'

His voice floated back down to her. 'Surprised you haven't already.'

The kitchen was small and compact. There was an oven, a two-burner hob and a small fridge. A microwave was securely wedged into a corner of the bench, and an electric toaster sat beside it. The contents of the kitchen cupboards told her he lived on tinned soup and toast.

She could do that too, but...

Glancing back towards the door, she tapped a finger against her lips. Everyone enjoyed a home-cooked meal. Wasn't there some saying about the way to a man's heart being through his stomach? She might not want to win his heart, but she did want to win his cooperation. And she'd become rather adept in the kitchen during the last three years.

She found strawberry jam in a cupboard, and a notepad under the newspaper, so she ate toast with jam and set about making two lists: one for the essentials she'd need and the other a grocery list. She checked the pots, pans and utensils. *Camelot* had everything she needed, all in pristine condition, which told a story of its own.

That done, she washed the few dishes, dried and put them away. She made more tea and handed Jude a mug, her arm emerging up the steps and through the door while she managed to keep the rest of herself hidden.

'Thanks.'

She might not be able to see his face, but she heard the surprise in his voice. Well, there had to be a couple of perks to having another person on board. When he was driving the boat he couldn't very well duck down to make tea whenever he wanted. She'd be more than happy to play tea lady.

With mug in hand, she moved along the corridor that opened onto Jude's bedroom with its neat double bed covered with a navy duvet. The room smelled of leather and the sea, like Jude himself.

The corridor narrowed again with two doors opening to her left. The first revealed a tiny toilet, the next a compact shower room. And then the corridor opened into another bedroom with bunk beds. One of the beds was made up with a sky-blue duvet. Cleverly constructed cupboards had been created in the rest of the available space, and several boxes rested along the wall—canned food, toilet paper, long-life milk and a box of yellow legal pads. There was a box of books too. Finally, a set of steps led up to the door leading out to the small deck at the front of the boat.

She mentally measured the space between bed, door and wall. If she moved a couple of boxes, she'd have enough room to do some yoga and other bits and pieces. It'd help keep her sane while confined on board. That was something. She *could* do this.

Back in the living area, she surveyed the space where she'd initially fallen through the door. The sweetest cast-iron wood burner rested in the far corner; the chimney disappearing through the roof was shiny, as if it was regularly scrubbed. A neat stack of wood rested in a box beside it.

Opposite the wood burner was that single arm chair, a foot rest and a small table—a space for one lone traveller. And, of course, more of those cleverly constructed cupboards and shelves. She slid back onto a bench at the dinette, refusing to invade what was clearly *his* space.

The light momentarily dimmed, as if they were travelling under a bridge or through an aqueduct. It would've been insanely interesting to go up and see, except she was currently too scared even to twitch a curtain at the windows. Going up on deck was out of the question. Maybe in a few days' time, when London was far behind. But, then again, maybe not.

She checked over the lists she'd made. She read the paper from cover to cover. She turned to the puzzle page to do the crossword and the sudoku.

Except...what if Jude did the puzzles? She'd stolen onto his boat. She wasn't going to steal his puzzles too. For all she knew, they might be the highlight of his day.

A pile of papers sat on the bench beside her. She seized yesterday's paper and turned to the puzzle page. He *did* do the puzzles—all of them. Of course he did; what else was there to do on a narrow boat?

When lunchtime finally rolled round, she made him thick roast-beef sandwiches and handed them up the steps. Again, she heard surprise in his 'Thanks.'

She ate her sandwich in silence. She resisted the urge to try and make conversation with him, though it settled in her bones like an ache. Jude didn't strike her as the chatty sort, and she'd be a model passenger if it killed her. Dropping her head to the table, she mumbled, 'It's going to kill me.'

She tidied the kitchen again.

An hour later she called up the stairs, 'Would it be okay if I read one of the books in the box in the—' she settled on '—spare bedroom?'

He didn't answer immediately. She swallowed. What was she going to do if he said no? Yoga; she'd do yoga. A lot of yoga.

'Sure.'

'Thank you.'

Racing down to her bedroom before he could change his mind, she carefully prised open one flap and then the other, discovering an almost entire set of 'Jason Diamond' books by Jasper Ballimore—a famously reclusive author who shunned live appearances, television interviews and the public eye. She stared at the books and grinned. A bit of Jason Diamond's kick-ass attitude was exactly what she needed.

Seizing the book on top, she dislodged the receipt and it fluttered to the floor. Reaching to place it back in the box, she glanced at the brief scrawl scratched across the bottom of it in big dark letters.

*If you're going to continue in this ridiculous seclusion, Jude, at least drop signed copies into bookshops along your route. Randomly signed Jasper Ballimore books are treasured by fans and will keep interest alive.*

There was a PS.

> *When can I expect the next book? It was*
> *due three months ago!!! Give me something*
> *to work with here, Jude.*

She dropped the note back into the box as if it had burned her. *Jude* was Jasper Ballimore? Oh, my God, that wasn't a secret he'd want her knowing! Her heart thundered. *Okay, all right, get a grip.* She was an actress, wasn't she?

Except she hadn't trained as an actress. Playing a part in front of a camera was very different from pretending to be something she wasn't in front of real people about real things in real life.

Fine! Hauling in a breath, she closed her eyes. She'd simply wipe this moment from her mind, never think about it again.

Folding the note, she tucked it down the side of the box before settling on the surprisingly comfortable bunk bed and cracking open the cover. She lost herself to the story for a happy hour, before once again chafing at the enforced inactivity. She wasn't used to being so *still* and it meant the same ugly thoughts kept circling her mind like sharks. Had she tested Margot's patience too far? Did Margot now hate her? Could she fix this?

She always came back to the same conclusion: lie low for the next two and a half weeks and allow the media speculation to die down. That way, Margot's big day wouldn't be marred by the paparazzi wanting to snap pictures of Cleo. They'd want to snap pictures of the bride instead, and the proud father of the bride, prominent politician Michael Milne. The bridesmaid would remain firmly in the background. Cleo crossed her fingers.

Mid-afternoon, Jude moored *Camelot*. She heard him tying off and, well, whatever else one did when mooring in a canal. She pulled herself into immediate straight lines.

*Don't talk his ear off. Don't ask him for anything unnecessary. Don't be a pain. And definitely don't remember that he's Jasper Ballimore!*

When he appeared, she sent him the smallest of smiles and slid out from behind the table. Rookie mistake, because space on the narrow boat was at a premium, and it shrank alarmingly when she and Jude were both standing in the galley.

She moistened her lips. 'Is there anything I can do?'

'Nope.'

'More tea or…?'

She broke off eyeing the flask he had tucked under one arm and the lunch box he held in his hand. As if in a dream, she reached for them. The lunch box held untouched sandwiches and a couple of biscuits. The flask was full of tea.

'It doesn't matter, Cleo.'

Oh, God, had her face fallen? She wrinkled

her nose. 'And here I was congratulating myself on being helpful.'

He took the lunch box, removed the biscuits and set the sandwiches in the fridge. 'No harm done. They'll keep till tomorrow.'

Clutching the flask, she slid back behind the table. 'This won't.' She poured herself a mug. It was still steaming hot. He slid his mug across and she filled it too.

He didn't sit. 'If it's any consolation, your sandwiches taste better than mine.'

She stared down her nose at him.

'You put hot English mustard on them.'

She'd found some in the cupboard.

'I forgot what a good combination that was. Who knew hot English mustard could make such a difference?'

Her heart gave a funny little twist. What else had he forgotten during his *ridiculous seclusion*?

*None of your business.*

She gestured to the door. 'Where are we?'

'Uxbridge.'

Uxbridge? *Uxbridge?* She could get from Maida Vale to Uxbridge in an hour on the tube; she could probably cycle it in under two hours. She made herself smile. 'Great.'

He leaned back against the bench, crossing his legs at the ankles. 'You're a terrible liar.'

She grimaced. 'I had no idea cruising the canal

was so leisurely. I thought we'd at least be in Oxford by now.'

His lips twitched. She thought it'd be kind of nice to see them break into a full-blown smile.

'There's been a bit of traffic in the canal.'

*On New Year's Day?*

'Slows things up.' He sipped his tea. 'You were hoping to be out of London by now.'

It was a statement, not a question. She shrugged. 'I suppose so, in an ideal world. But, as long as I stay below and out of sight, it doesn't really matter where I am, does it?'

Jude eyed Cleo over his mug, trying to work her out. She was doing her best to be low maintenance—not to make a fuss or be a bother—but she was keyed up tighter than an anchor winch.

*Think it might have something to do with the fact her picture appeared on the front page of the newspaper today? Or that her lying scumbag of a boyfriend cheated on her? Or that her Bridezilla of a sister was throwing hissy fits?*

Even he had to admit the woman had a lot going on. And, in spite of it all, she was holding up pretty well. *And* she'd gone to the trouble of putting hot English mustard on his sandwich. He didn't know why that caught at him, only that it did.

'If it's any consolation—' he shrugged '—I hate London too.'

She waved both arms towards the door. 'What on earth are you doing here, then, when you've a whole network of canals at your fingertips.'

He tried not to scowl. 'My grandmother's funeral.'

She froze, a stricken expression in her eyes, and he immediately wished the stark words unsaid. Cleo might be a total mess, but she didn't deserve his bitterness. 'Don't look like that. You weren't to know.' He tried to shrug, but the movement was jerky. 'As executor of her will, I've had to remain and settle her estate.'

Her eyes filled. 'Oh, Jude, I'm so very sorry.'

Her sincerity almost undid him. He needed a change of topic…fast.

'You check out your sleeping quarters yet?' The boat was a reverse configuration, with the sleeping quarters in the bow rather than the stern.

She nodded. 'Your boat is amazing.'

His cup halted halfway to his mouth.

'I mean, it's not very wide.'

He lowered his mug. 'Less than seven feet.' Six feet ten inches, to be precise. Reaching up, he touched the ceiling. 'Six feet six inches high.'

For a moment her gaze rested on him, weighted with something that had an invisible hand reaching out to squeeze the air from his body. Shaking herself, she glanced away. Air rushed back into his lungs.

'The design is clever, each nook and cranny

designed for maximum storage. Like I said—
amazing.'

'And your bed?'

'Comfortable.'

She really wasn't going to be a prima donna
about this? 'It's tiny and cramped.'

'I might not manage a full yoga routine in there
but, as you promised me a bed and not a yoga
studio...'

Her eyes danced. He resisted the urge to smile
back and wondered how long her good behaviour would last. 'You'll have more privacy down
there. I'll pin a sheet up in the doorway of your
bedroom later.'

'I don't want you going to any trouble.'

'No trouble.' It was as much for his peace of
mind as hers. He didn't want to catch a glimpse
of a naked leg or...

He shook away the images that flicked through
his mind, but not fast enough. His skin tightened
as if it had grown too small for him. A throb
started up deep inside. *This* was why he didn't
want her—or anyone—on board *Camelot*. He
wanted peace and quiet...

*'You're hiding from life.'*

He straightened as his grandmother's words
sounded through him, glaring at his feet. 'Did
you make a list of the things I need to get you?'

She wordlessly handed him a sheet of paper.

His brows shot up at the first item on her list. 'A tape measure?'

'If I'm not going to my final bridesmaid fitting, then I need to make sure my measurements don't change too much. If they do, I can send the dress maker the new measurements.'

He stared.

She rolled her shoulders. 'A bridesmaid has certain responsibilities. I've let Margot down enough. From now on, nothing but perfection will do.'

He opened his mouth. He closed it again.

'I'm not going to starve myself, if that's what you're worried about, but nor am I going to gorge myself on doughnuts.'

She liked doughnuts?

He went back to her list: toothbrush, yoga pants, T-shirts…underwear. His nose curled.

'What? It's the phone, isn't it? I know it's a hassle, but I put all the details there and—'

'The phone is a piece of cake.' He pointed to the offending item. 'I've never bought ladies' underwear in my life. How am I going to find the…?'

She gazed at him blankly.

'The right kind?' He'd walked past the women's lingerie section in department stores. It was bigger than the entire men's clothing section!

She pressed her lips together, as if trying not to laugh. 'It's easy-peasy. I only wear silk and lace.'

*What the hell…?*

'They're about this big.' She held her finger and

thumb about two inches apart. 'And they come in a colour called rose blush—'

He choked and she broke off, laughing. 'I'm pulling your leg, Jude. I didn't think you'd take me seriously.' Her grin widened. 'You should've seen your face.'

*I'd rather not, thanks all the same.* Joke or no joke, he now couldn't get the image of Cleo wearing nothing more than a scrap of silk and lace the same colour as her lips out of his mind. He shouldn't be imagining Cleo practically naked. And he sure as hell shouldn't be thinking about her lips.

Intellectually, he'd known that Cleo was attractive—he'd seen a few episodes of the show she'd starred in and had seen the headlines of her many scandals. But in the flesh Cleo was more beguiling than he'd have credited. She vibrated with life. *She sparkled.*

None of it changed the fact that she was the last person he'd ever get involved with. He didn't court scandal. He preferred to live his life out of the limelight, thank you very much.

'You can get all the things on my list at a department store, or even a supermarket.'

He glanced back at her list.

'You don't need to go anywhere fancy. The underwear will come in a pack of five.' She reached across and pointed. The scent of pears filled his nostrils—fresh, sweet and oddly innocent.

'I've written the details here—bikini briefs, a hundred percent cotton. But full brief, boy leg, trunks will all do too.'

She'd written all of that down, as if aware the ladies' underwear department might bamboozle him. He needed to stop making mountains out of molehills. 'Colour preferences?'

'Don't care two jots.'

Obviously she was determined to keep up the low-maintenance masquerade.

He tapped the final item on her list. 'Puzzle book?'

'It's important to keep the mind active.'

His gaze slid to the paper.

'I didn't do your puzzles. I checked the papers from earlier in the week and saw that you did them.'

Her thoughtfulness slid under his guard. 'You could've done the puzzles, Cleo. I wouldn't have minded.'

'Seemed presumptuous—not my paper. And puzzles can be a routine thing. You might settle in after dinner with a nice cup of cocoa and unwind by doing the puzzles.'

She had him nailed.

*I know people.*

Maybe she did. 'Substitute that mug of cocoa for a dram of whisky, and you just about hit the nail on the head.'

She bit her lip. 'I made another list. I hope it's not presumptuous but, Jude, I love to cook.'

She handed him another sheet of paper—a shopping list!

'I thought I'd make a lasagne for dinner tonight, if that's okay with you.'

'Lasagne?' he parroted stupidly. The papers always made out that Cleo was a high-maintenance, spoiled starlet. And, while he appreciated the lack of foot-stomping about the size of her bedroom, he found it a stretch too far that she was now offering to cook. Next she'd be offering to knit him a scarf!

*She's an actress. She's probably buttering you up so you'll let her stay for another week.*

'I know it's not diet food, but it'll only be a small one. You can have the leftovers for lunch tomorrow, if you want.' She wrinkled her nose. 'I'm in the mood for comfort food.'

Her expression had his chest clenching.

*Actress, remember?*

'And I've made a list of ingredients for a stir fry for tomorrow night. I checked the size of your fridge and we should be able to fit that lot in.'

'You don't need to cook, Cleo.'

'I want to, honestly.'

More likely a case of seeing his cupboards were stacked with nothing but tinned food. He rolled his shoulders. There was nothing wrong with tinned food. And yet the thought of home-cooked lasagne had his mouth watering. *If* she could cook...

'Besides, it'll give me something to do.'

She held her credit card out to him, but he raised both hands, warding her off.

'But—'

'Getting caught with your credit card and going down for credit card fraud?' He shook his head. 'No thanks. Besides, that could blow your cover.'

She swore. 'Then I want an itemised account. You need to bring all the receipts back with you.' She pointed a surprisingly fierce finger at him. 'I want to see *all* the receipts.'

It was novel not to be expected to pick up the bill—a fact that would undoubtedly change if she found out who he was. 'Deal,' he said, seizing his phone and keys.

Her hands twisted together and she suddenly looked young and vulnerable, as if he were her only friend in the world and she was about to lose him. He bit back something short and succinct. At the moment, he *was* the only person who knew where she was; the only person who seemed to care about the plight she was in. She might be a celebrity, but that didn't make her invulnerable. It didn't shield her from grief or heartache.

'Will you be okay while I'm gone?'

She pasted on a too-bright smile that made his eyes ache. 'Absolutely! Is there anything I need to know, or do?'

He shook his head. 'We're tied up safe and sound, but there are narrow boats moored either end of us. Don't answer if anyone knocks. And keep the noise down.'

'Roger.'

It took him off-guard, how much he hated leaving her on her own. *Crazy.* She'd be as safe as houses, provided she stayed put and out of sight.

'Look, provided I can negotiate the ladies' underwear department without too many hassles, I shouldn't be gone longer than an hour.'

Her eyes danced then. 'Good luck with that. And don't worry about me; I'll be fine.'

Of course she would. He nodded at the paper. 'Do the puzzles. I'll grab another paper while I'm out.'

It took Jude two hours. When he clattered back on board, Cleo jumped up and rushed across to take bags from him.

'What on earth…? Did you leave anything in the shops for the rest of the people?'

'Very funny.' He shoved a bag of fresh doughnuts at her.

She stared at them, then back at him. Her eyes grew suspiciously bright. 'You bought me doughnuts?'

'Comfort food. Won't happen again. Dieting again after today,' he muttered, easing past to set the shopping on the kitchen bench.

She slid into the bench seat, facing him. She stared at the doughnuts as if they were diamonds. He rolled his shoulders. They were just doughnuts. Didn't the people in her life do nice things for her?

*Her boyfriend cheated on her. Her sister is making ridiculous demands of her. And her father...?* Who knew what the deal was with her father?

'Why are you scowling?'

He jumped, making the scowl comical. 'I have three words for you, Cleo: ladies'...underwear... department.'

She laughed. In this light, her eyes were the colour of sea mist—*really* pretty. And when they danced they could steal a man's breath.

'Was it dire?'

'The sales lady thought me a pervert. She didn't believe me when I said the underwear was for my little sister.'

'Do you have a little sister?'

'Well...no.'

'If you had the same expression on your face then as you do now, then she'd have known you were lying.'

'See?' He lifted his hands. 'I told you she thought me a pervert!'

Another laugh gurgled out of her. It made him feel good, as if he'd done a good thing. He nodded at the bags in front of her. 'Phone, yoga pants,

T-shirts, hoody, PJs. Check and make sure they're all okay.'

He upended a bag of pears he'd bought into a bowl. Lifting one to his nose, he inhaled its scent. *Heaven.*

'What's this?'

*Damn.* He dropped the pear to reach across and pluck the boutique bag from her fingers. 'I…uh… it was supposed to be a joke—make you laugh.' He rolled his shoulders. 'But now it feels pervy.'

Her brows shot up. She eased out from behind the table to stand in front of him. 'Intrigued now.'

With a curse, he shoved the bag into her hands, scowling. 'Joke, remember?'

She pulled out a package wrapped in tissue paper and unfolded it. He winced at the tiny rose silk-and-cream lace panties that dangled from her fingers.

God, what would she think of him…?

Clutching them to her chest, Cleo roared. She bent at the waist as if unable to contain her mirth and literally *roared* with laughter. Tears poured down her face. Straightening, she tried to speak, but one glance at him sent her into fresh gales. She had to hold onto the table to stop from falling to the floor. Collapsing on her back on the bench seat of the dinette, her feet kicked the air, her entire body convulsing and her face crinkling.

*With laughter.* Something in his chest wrenched free and he found himself grinning.

'You braved a Victoria's Secret store?' Pushing upright, she stood again, mopping at her eyes. 'I can't believe you did that. I wish I could've seen your face.'

'I should've gone there in the first place. The staff just took it in their stride—proper professionals.'

She hiccupped another laugh. 'I didn't think anything would be able to make me laugh today.'

His heart pounded against his ribs too hard.

'Best joke present ever, Jude.'

*Really?*

'You're a gem. Thank you.'

Reaching across, she hugged him. She was all soft, warm woman, and she hugged him as if she really meant it. He couldn't remember the last time... Everything inside him started to ache.

Letting him go, she slid back into her seat and pulled the doughnuts towards her. 'Doughnut?'

He dragged air into cramped lungs. 'No thanks; I'm having a pear.'

# CHAPTER THREE

CLEO WATCHED JUDE fork the tiniest amount of lasagne into his mouth, as if he didn't trust that she could actually cook. One bite, and his face cleared, and then he tucked in as if he hadn't eaten in a week.

Something stupid caught low in her belly. He looked as if he hadn't had a home-cooked meal in *forever*. She was suddenly and fiercely glad she'd offered to cook, and beyond the fact that it had given her something to do.

He glanced up, his gaze pinning her to her seat. 'Everything okay?'

'No.' The word blurted out before she could stop it. The joke panties were to blame, and the doughnuts. They'd changed everything. She didn't want to lie to him. He deserved better.

'I know you're Jasper Ballimore.'

He froze.

'There was a note from your publisher in the box of books.'

He set his cutlery down with one succinct and very rude word.

'Your secret is safe with me—I promise. But it's a big secret, and you'll want to protect yourself. Have your lawyer send me something—a non-disclosure or confidentiality agreement—and I'll sign it. I won't tell a soul.' *Please don't throw me off your narrow boat.* 'It's just—'

'What?'

The word was barked from him and she could feel herself shrivel. 'It just seemed wrong to feign ignorance.'

His glare didn't ease.

She closed her eyes. 'Do you want me to leave?'

'So you can run off to the press?'

Her eyes snapped open. 'You think that's what I'd do?'

He remained silent.

Her sinuses burned. 'Oh, that's right—I'm *that* girl. The train wreck, the car crash, the wild child who'll do *anything* for attention. The kind of person who takes delight in wrecking lives for the fun of it.'

Their gazes clashed. He grimaced. 'That's not what I meant.'

'That's exactly what you meant!' Her hand clenched, but she didn't slam it on the table as she wanted to. 'I thought you of all people would understand.'

'Me?'

'Yes, *you*!' She lowered her voice and spoke in a whisper. 'As Jasper B you guard your identity jealously, do everything you can to avoid publicity. I thought that meant you understood the half-truths and lies the media feed on—the twisted version of reality they peddle. I thought you were safeguarding yourself against it so you could focus on the writing rather than the celebrity. And I thought that meant you'd be able to see beneath the lies they printed about people like me.'

All the good things inside her—the things that had kept her going for the day, the tiny threads of hope and optimism—all dissolved.

'You're a writer. I thought you'd have more *imagination*.' Seizing her fork, she stabbed a piece of rocket. 'But you're just like everyone else.'

'Cleo...'

She sent him a tight smile. 'Silly me.'

Jude's hands clenched and unclenched on either side of his plate. 'Everything you just said is true. I'm sorry.'

She stared back stonily.

'*Really* sorry.'

She swallowed and glanced away.

'I've been operating under too many mistaken assumptions where you're concerned, which isn't only unfair but stupid,' he said. 'I should never have made that crack about you going to the press.

If that had been your plan, you wouldn't have told me about your discovery in the first place.'

He looked haggard, as if he loathed himself. It was a hundred times worse than his previous scowl.

'I've no defence other than the fact you caught me off-guard. I panicked. My unmasking was the last thing I expected today.'

She suspected *she* was the last thing he'd expected today. He'd made an error of judgement, but he wasn't the only one. He didn't deserve to go to the gallows over it. 'Forget about it,' she mumbled. 'I can get on a bit of a soapbox about it.'

'With some cause.'

She shook her head. 'I've not always made good decisions. I can't blame the press for that. Besides, you don't know me. For all you knew, I could've been about to try and extort money from you.'

He stared.

'It happened to me once.'

'How? Who?'

'An ex-boyfriend. He'd taken photos of me without my permission.' Naked photos.

His Adam's apple bobbed. 'And those photos were published, weren't they?'

'Well, I refused to be blackmailed.' It was also the moment she'd decided she was done with the whole celebrity scene. 'I did sue, however.' And the money she'd been awarded had paid for her website development training. She rolled her eyes; and more therapy.

'Cleo…'

'Apology accepted, Jude.'

He opened his mouth and then closed it; nodded.

'So…' Picking up her cutlery again, she tried for light-hearted and breezy. 'Jason Diamond is your creation, huh? That's pretty amazing.'

Jason Diamond was one of the most beloved fictional characters of modern times. One of the good guys—ex-law enforcement and reluctant hero, he stood on the side of the weak and underprivileged, fighting for those who couldn't fight for themselves. Justice could be his middle name.

He glanced up and shook his head. 'Don't make that particular mistake. I'm nothing like JD.'

She went back to her lasagne and salad. 'JD is always helping damsels and dudes in distress—just like you helped me.'

'I didn't jump in front of a bullet for you.'

He shrugged, as if saving her from the press hadn't been particularly noteworthy. She stopped eating and frowned. Had his shoulders been that broad earlier? Dragging her gaze away, she focussed on cutting her food, lifting it to her mouth and chewing.

*Keep things light.*

'You might be asked to take that bullet if I screw up again and ruin Margot's wedding.'

A corner of his mouth twitched. 'You're not going to ruin Margot's wedding. She's just stressed. Brides get stressed. It's a thing.'

'A...*thing*?' She raised an eyebrow. 'You have experience?'

'I'm a writer.'

He shrugged again and she could've groaned. Every time he did that it drew her attention to the breadth of those annoyingly *broad* shoulders. Her fingers tightened around her cutlery.

'I do my due diligence; squirrel odd snippets of information away. Believe me, stressed brides are a thing.'

She leaned towards him. 'Are you going to have a stressed bride in your next book? That could...'

She gulped back the rest of her words, recalling his publisher's note. He obviously wasn't writing. And reminding him of that wasn't in the spirit of model-passenger behaviour.

'Thank you for letting me cook tonight.'

He frowned. 'Why are you thanking me? I should be thanking you.'

She sliced a cherry tomato in half. 'I really do like to cook.' It was one of the two things that kept her on the straight and narrow—exercise and cooking. 'And cooking dinner made me feel as if...'

'What?'

'As if I was pulling my weight a bit. Making up in a small way for thrusting my presence on you.'

He pointed his knife at her. 'You're paying me, remember? *And* you traded your sunnies.'

She tried to look casual, or at least not stricken. 'Oh, in that case, you got a bargain.'

'Did you see I grabbed you another pair while I was out?'

*Had he?* Abandoning her food, she rifled through the bags still sitting on the bench, her hand eventually emerging with the sunglasses. She put them on. They felt wrong, but they covered her eyes at the front and sides—great disguise sunglasses. 'How do they look?'

'Very chic.'

Smiling, she took them off and set them on the table. 'Thank you.'

'You want to tell me why you're so attached to those ugly things you were wearing earlier?'

'You want to talk about the next JD book?'

He pursed his lips. *'Touché.'* Then he pinned her to her seat with a ferocious glare. 'Is Margot worth it—all the sacrifices you're making?'

She went hot all over and then cold. When she realised she clutched her cutlery as if it was a weapon, she forced herself to loosen her grip. 'Yes.'

They ate in silence after that.

A short while later, Jude shook himself. 'I bought a bottle of wine. Would you like a glass?'

'No, thank you.' She eyed him carefully, moistening her lips. 'I don't drink.'

He held her gaze. 'Alcoholic?'

'No. At least, I don't think so. It's just, when I drink, my guard lowers and I'm more likely to do something impulsive.'

'Something you'll regret?'

'Usually something that will cause my family pain and, or, maximum embarrassment.' Such as appearing on the front page of the newspaper having an altercation with her jerk of a boyfriend. *Ex-boyfriend.*

'And, before you ask, I wasn't drinking last night. Clayton just…'

'Got under your skin?'

She should've walked away. But then he'd said that dreadful thing and she'd seen red.

'Stop beating yourself up about it, Cleo.'

*Easier said than done.*

Jude finished his lasagne. She stood and reached for his plate. 'You want more?'

'Is there more?' He eyed the leftovers, watching as she cut him another generous slice. 'There's enough left for dinner tomorrow night.'

'I don't like having the same thing two nights running,' she informed him. If his expression was anything to go by, that wasn't an issue for him. 'Breakfast and lunch, I don't care. Dinner, I like to mix up. Which means there's enough here for you to have seconds now and for lunch tomorrow too if you want.'

time.' She forced herself to meet his gaze. 'She didn't deserve that.'

'And yet she forgave you.'

For which she'd always be grateful. 'When I sobered up, I was appalled at what I'd done. I grovelled for days, begged her to forgive me.'

She'd been so ashamed. She still was.

'Margot laid down the law—said I had to go to rehab. I agreed. I wasn't doing drugs, but nobody believed that at the time, and I *was* drinking too much. So off to rehab I went. She also said I had to get counselling. I did, and it helped. That's the point when I started turning my life around.'

'And maybe she thinks losing that job is a small sacrifice to pay to have her sister well and healthy.'

'She probably does. She's a good soul. But you have to see, after all of that, I can't ruin her wedding too. I can't cast *any* shadow over it. All eyes should be on her, not me. Her focus should be on marrying the man of her dreams, not getting me out of another mess.'

Was Brett the man of Margot's dreams, though? As Margot's bridesmaid, not to mention her sister, it was her duty to make sure of that, wasn't it? And how could she do that when she was stuck on a narrow boat in the middle of nowhere? Her lips twisted. Unlike her, though, Margot was smart. *Be more like Margot.*

'I want,' he said as she slid the plate in front of him. 'It's great.'

'May I?' She held up a pear.

'Knock yourself out. Help yourself to anything you want. It's part of the deal.'

She sat again, sliced and cored the pear, her mind going over the question Jude had asked—was Margot worth the sacrifices she was making? She suspected he was more like his fictional creation than he cared to admit. He saw her as a damsel in distress and Margot as a villain. That couldn't be further from the truth and she needed to disabuse him of the notion. She didn't want him concocting some Jason Diamond scheme to win her justice. He'd be fighting for the wrong side.

'You think Margot is the bad guy in all of this, but you couldn't be more mistaken if you tried.'

He stopped mid-chew.

'Margot is worth ten of me. And I owe her.'

He finished his mouthful slowly. 'You sure you don't want that glass of wine?'

'Positive, but don't let that stop you.'

He rose and poured himself a glass of red. 'Look…' He slid back into his seat. 'Just because you were a little wild when you were younger…'

'I was charged with being drunk and disorderly twice. I was photographed dancing half-naked in the fountain in Trafalgar Square!'

'Not your finest hour.' He pointed his fork at her. 'But it doesn't make you a bad person.'

'And that's before we throw in the series of disastrous relationships I've had with high-profile men.' With last night's fiasco being her crowning glory.

'Again, it doesn't make you a bad person.'

But it did make her a delusional one—or maybe she was just a slow learner. She dreamed of creating the warm, family environment her mother had. To date, though, she could never have made that dream a reality with the men she'd sought to find it with. She'd just been too blind to see it.

Swearing off men for the foreseeable future wasn't only her wisest course of action, it was the *only* course of action that made sense. Until she could make better decisions where men were concerned, she was avoiding all romance, full-stop.

*No men. No romance. No making headlines.*

She took her time eating a slice of pear. 'Do you know what Margot's dream was, before she decided to follow my father into politics?'

He rolled his shoulders. 'This isn't any of my business, Cleo.'

'She wanted to work for the United Nations. She made it through the first and second rounds of testing, and the first lot of interviews. The next hurdle was another interview. The powers that be decided at six p.m. the night before that it'd take place in the family home at seven-thirty a.m.—apparently they like to take you off-guard and

make things stressful to see how you perform under pressure.'

Jude rubbed a hand over his face, as if sensing this story didn't have a happy ending.

'I stumbled in at seven forty-five after a night out, still drunk.' For God's sake, who stumbled home drunk at practically eight in the morning? 'And I proceeded to tell all assembled that Margot was a saint, and that perhaps she'd missed her calling as a nun.' Acid burned her throat. She'd been so angry at the world. 'I said her perfection was annoying and called them all a bunch of smug do-gooders who deserved each other.'

Jude swirled the wine in his glass. 'I'm guessing she didn't get the job.'

'No.' She couldn't look at him. 'It's the wo[rst] thing I've ever done.' She'd *never* forgive hers[elf] for it, not for as long as she lived. 'I was so [sis]ter. So lost after our mother died.'

Their mother had been the machine tha[t] kept the family running. Cleo had only bee[n sev]enteen when she'd died. Margot had been t[wenty-] two. Cleo had been twenty-two when she'd [ruined] Margot's dream.

'Apparently, I wanted to make everyone [mis]erable as I was.' And in that instance s[he'd suc]ceeded. 'I resented Margot for being so [per]perfect and doing no wrong, even wh[en at the] time she was hauling me out of trouble[.]

'It's not too much for her to ask me to keep a low profile for the next two and a half weeks.'

He blew out a breath and nodded. 'I guess not.'

'You asked me if she's worth it—she's worth my every best effort.'

He leaned back, his shoulders sagging as if he'd just lost a fight. Except they hadn't been fighting, had they?

He tapped a fist to his mouth. He had firm, lean lips and she found her gaze riveted to them. A woman could weave fantasies around a mouth like that...

She tore her gaze away. *For God's sake!* She had to stop this. She had to stop making such terrible mistakes. She would *not* start fantasising about a man she barely knew.

'If we're going to successfully hide you for a fortnight...'

She blinked, and then her every muscle electrified. 'A fortnight? Did you just say...?'

His lips twisted, as if he were mocking himself. 'I think we both know I'm going to let you stay for as long as you need to.'

She could hug him! Except, she'd already done that and it had been a huge mistake. Plus, she was only making *good* decisions from hereon in. 'I'll pay you.'

He was a successful writer—*really* successful—but she'd read somewhere that writers didn't actually make all that much money.

'You'll pay me what we've already agreed and take over the cooking for the duration of the trip.'

She opened her mouth to argue.

'That's the deal—take it or leave it.'

Snapping her mouth shut, she dragged in a breath. She'd have to find some other way to repay him. 'I'll take it. And, Jude, thank you.'

He scowled and shrugged.

'I mean it. You're a lifesaver.'

'I'm a moron,' he muttered, making her laugh.

'Why?' Cleo fixed Jude with a gaze he couldn't read. 'Why are you helping me? I know you're a decent guy and all, but I also know you wish me a million miles away.'

She looked so alone and his heart gave a sick kick. She was used to everyone expecting something from her, wanting a piece of her. He suspected Cleo didn't get favours for free; they'd always come with a price tag attached. Was it any wonder she wanted to know what price she'd be asked to pay for the privilege of remaining aboard *Camelot*?

Exhaustion pounded at him. He uttered words he'd have not expected to say to her in a million years. 'Nine months ago, I lost my brother—car accident.'

Her quick intake of breath speared into his chest. 'Oh, God... Jude.'

'If I could do anything to bring him back, I would.'

She scrubbed both hands over her face.

'If you cry, I'm kicking you off *Camelot*.'

It was an idle threat, but she buried her head in her hands and took a ragged breath before pulling them away again, her eyes dry. 'You know how important Margot is to me because that's how important your brother was to you.'

*Something like that.* His nostrils flared as the familiar grief rose through him. He glared. 'We're not talking about this any more.'

'Okay.'

There'd just been too much loss. He didn't want to face any more, not even as a bystander.

Jude rose early the next day. He'd not slept well, too aware of another person occupying space on his boat, finding sanctuary on *Camelot*, just as he had. And he was still reeling from the fact that he'd allowed it to happen at all. He might not have been hard-nosed enough to escort Cleo off *Camelot* into the waiting arms of the journalists, but to let her stay for longer than an hour…

His hands fisted. Coming face to face with Elodie, his late brother's wife, at his grandmother's funeral had opened wounds that had barely had the chance to heal. God only knew why, but it had thrown him and left him feeling bruised. When

Cleo had crashed onto his boat, his defences had been down.

He cast off at first light. Peering into the mild early-morning light, he could admit to himself that he didn't regret letting her stay, not really. What he'd started to doubt were his motives. Helping Cleo wouldn't erase the events of the past. It wouldn't give him absolution. It would, however, provide him with distraction.

And yesterday morning, sitting at the table, trying to read the paper, distraction was exactly what he'd craved. He'd wanted to drive Elodie's bitter words from his mind, if only for an hour.

And now Cleo was here, all warm, lovely woman, trying her best not to be a nuisance, and that had slid beneath his guard in ways he hadn't expected. Her sparkly chatter, her easy frankness and irrepressible humour were balm to a starving soul.

Which was stupid, and wrong. Because, first, he didn't deserve balm; and, second, unlike his fictional creation Jason Diamond—who in Jude's more optimistic moments he'd once considered his shadow soul—his motives weren't pure. In searching for distraction, he was in danger of using Cleo.

When he added his growing attraction to her—because, damn, Cleo was pretty with her dark hair, that classic English rose complexion and those extraordinary green eyes—it had the potential to lead him to places he had no right to go to.

She was a woman in need. She was vulnerable. His hand tightened on the tiller. He would *not* take advantage of her.

'Good morning.'

Cleo peered up at him blearily from the bottom of the steps, blinking sleep from her eyes.

'Do you know what time it is?'

'Sorry, I wanted to get an early start. I want to put some distance between us and London today.'

She smothered a yawn. 'Good idea. Do you have your flask with you or would you like a coffee?'

'No flask. I was hoping to rely on your good nature. I'd kill for a coffee.'

A few minutes later, she handed him up a steaming mug and sat in his easy chair to sip her own. From there, if she ducked down a little she could peer up at him, and if he ducked a little he could glance down at her. She looked ridiculously cute in her flannel pyjamas—deliberately chosen by him to cover her from head to toe. She wasn't supposed to look sexy in them.

He ground his teeth together. She *didn't* look sexy in them. 'Sleep well?' He didn't glance down. He didn't want to see those generous lips curve into a smile if she answered in the affirmative or that cute nose crinkle in a grimace if she answered in the negative.

'I never sleep well the first night in a new place.'

Had her nose crinkled? He glanced down. Nope, her face was smooth. She'd drawn her feet up onto the chair, a pair of his socks on her feet, because he'd realised last night that she'd forgotten to put socks on her list of things for him to buy. He'd hunted her out a pair of his own. They looked better on her than they did on him.

*They're just socks.*

'What can you see?'

Her words dragged him from his thoughts. He glanced around. 'There aren't many people around. Why don't you pull on my mac and a beanie and come up to see for yourself?' Nobody would recognise her in that get-up.

She shuddered and shook her head. 'Too risky.'

The story she'd confided to him last night—her guilt over ruining her sister's chance at a dream job—still chafed at him. He understood guilt. He understood wanting to make amends. He might never find redemption for himself, but he'd help Cleo keep her promise to Margot. Family meant everything—a fact he'd only discovered after losing his own.

He shook the sombre reflection away to focus on painting a picture for her with words. 'It's still and pretty. There's a fine mist rising from the water and the canal looks like a mirror. It's the colour of mercury tinged with a rosy glow at the edges.'

He fancied he heard her sigh.

'In summer, the plane trees are a bright green, but at the moment the branches are bare. And, while the sun is mild, it's sparkling off the dew, which makes the city look gilded...washed clean.'

'How pretty you make it sound.'

Speaking of sound... 'The morning is meeting with the birds' approval.'

'Oh, yes! They're singing their hearts out.'

Her smile... He forced his gaze back to the canal. 'There are a few narrow boats moored to our left, which is port. Starboard is to the right.'

She repeated that as it fixing it in her mind.

'Bow refers to the front, and the back—' he patted the railing behind him '—is the stern.'

She repeated that too.

'There's a canal path that runs both sides. To the left there's a brick wall, probably houses and shops behind it.'

He continued describing what he could see. She listened as if mesmerised. But he suspected that was a symptom of a lack of sleep and not enough caffeine in her system yet. He hadn't spoken for this length of time, uninterrupted, in an age. He found he didn't hate it.

'That was perfect!'

He blinked to find her beaming up at him. His pulse stuttered.

'You ought to be a writer.'

He knew she'd said it to make him laugh, but a black cloud threatened to descend.

'Also, I wasn't dissing your boat when I said I didn't sleep well. I'll sleep like a log tonight. I'll probably snore and keep you awake.'

He couldn't resist teasing her. 'You did that last night.'

'I did not!'

He bit back a grin. 'How'd you know?'

'Because, if I had, I'd have a sore throat now.'

'When *do* you snore?'

'When I have a cold, have had too much to drink or am over-tired.'

'Forewarned is forearmed. I have earplugs.'

She laughed and it blew away the threads of that black cloud. He wasn't entirely sure that was a good thing.

She made scrambled eggs for breakfast. He told her she didn't have to cook his breakfast. She said she was making it for herself and it was just as easy to make enough for two, which was hard to argue with. He ate it standing at the tiller.

Afterwards she disappeared for a while. He heard the shower running. He heard her wash the dishes, and then moving about, as if tidying up. She made tea—which he declined—and sat at the dinette doing things on her phone, probably sending texts and reading emails. And checking the newspaper sites to make sure she'd not appeared in any of them.

She did some stretches in the space beside the dinette, a few yoga poses and sit-ups. She walked the length of the narrow boat a few times. More than a few times... A lot of times...

After lunch—*damn that lasagne was good*—she sat in his chair with the crossword book he'd bought for her.

'Jude,' she called up, 'I'm looking for a five-letter word that means "to push forward". It ends in an L.'

'Impel?'

'Yes!'

They did three crosswords. At this rate, he'd need to stop somewhere and buy her another puzzle book. She disappeared again for a while; he thought she was taking a nap, but thumping vibrated from the front of the boat—something unfamiliar. 'Are you okay?' he called down the stairs.

No answer. Damn it! Was Cleo okay?

Easing into the bank, he threw the middle mooring rope over a bollard and tied off, before racing through the boat's very narrow corridor. The thumping hadn't stopped. He halted in the doorway to her bedroom and then rested his hands on his knees, relief pouring through him.

Cleo had her back to him, her phone in one hand, earbuds in her ears, dancing—in a headbanging style—to some playlist or other. Easing upright, he grinned. She gave a silly little shimmy before jumping and turning on the spot. She still didn't see him, though, as she had her eyes closed, her mouth moving silently to the words of the song. Then she froze and opened one eye, as if sensing him there.

Scrunching both eyes shut on a groan, she covered her face with her hands. Straightening, she pulled the earbuds from her ears and glared. 'I know this is your boat, but you're not allowed to sneak up on me.' She gestured around. 'Privacy, remember?'

'I called out but you didn't answer. I felt thumping. I was worried.'

Her cheeks went bright-pink.

'I thought you were stuck somewhere or had fallen or something.'

She groaned again, even louder.

His grin widened. 'It was quite a dance.'

'Hey!' She thumped his arm. 'I didn't know I had an audience. And I'm sorry if I worried you... made you pull over...'

'No probs.' It was time for a toilet break anyway. There were a lot of pros to his solitary cruising, but tying up whenever he needed to pee was not one of them.

'How do you do this?' She thumped down onto her bunk bed. 'How do you not go stir crazy?' She gestured. 'How do you keep so *fit*?'

'I go running, first thing in the morning and then again in the evening.'

'You didn't go running last night.'

'I had unexpected company.'

She blew out a breath and nodded.

She was bored and it was only day two. She'd be climbing walls by the end of two weeks. 'What do you do, Cleo?'

She stared at him blankly.

'During the day, when you're at home—what do you do?'

Her face cleared. 'I'm a freelance website designer. I've several jobs on the go at the moment. If I were at home, I'd be working on those.'

'What equipment do you need to do your work?'

'Just my laptop. It's got everything on it: the software I use, all of my clients' details, all the work I've done on the projects so far...'

'Is there someone who could have your laptop couriered somewhere for you?'

'My flatmate Jenna. We've been friends since... well...rehab days.'

'Do you trust her?'

'With my life.'

Cleo, he suspected, was far too trusting.

'Right, have her courier it to this address.'

Turning, he walked back to the galley, jotted an address down on a scrap of paper and handed it to her.

She stared at it and then at him. 'You're a life saver, you know that?'

His lips twisted. Yeah, he was a real knight in shining armour.

# CHAPTER FOUR

CLEO ARRANGED FOR her laptop to be sent to the address Jude had provided.

'All done,' she called up the steps.

'Excellent.'

That was it. He said nothing more. Of course he said nothing more—the man was a recluse. He enjoyed his solitude, solitude she'd so rudely disturbed. Her stomach churned.

*Don't bug him. Don't pester him with a thousand questions. Don't give him a reason to retract his offer.*

Nobody would think to look for her on Jude's narrow boat. *Camelot* was the perfect place to hide. She couldn't give him any reason to abandon her on the side of the canal.

Zipping her mouth very firmly closed, she reached for her Jason Diamond book and lost herself in its pages. She came to with a little bump a couple of hours later when they moored. Voices carried over the water, along with the low hum of traffic. Water lapped against the hull and somewhere nearby a lark sang. The lapping water and bird song was soothing. The sounds of traffic and people not so much.

'Where are we?' she asked when Jude descended inside.

'About quarter of a mile from Hemel Hempstead's town centre. Normally I'd moor at Apsley, but we made good time today.'

No doubt due to the early hour they'd set off this morning, and the cracking pace he'd kept up all day.

Those broad shoulders lifted. 'It's not far for me to duck out and grab a few things.'

She bit her tongue to stop from asking what *things*—none of her business.

'Need anything?'

She shook her head. He stared at her for a long moment and it made her fidget.

*Don't frown at the poor man.* Instead, she pasted on a bright smile that made him blink. Too much? Ugh. Why could she never get that balance right?

'Thanks for checking, but I've everything I need. We've all the ingredients for dinner. And, if we're stopping in Berkhamsted tomorrow, I'm guessing I can grab a few additional things then if I need to.'

'What shoe size are you?'

She frowned, even though she wasn't supposed to frown. *'Why?'*

He merely raised an eyebrow and she threw up her hands. 'A four, but—'

'Can I get you to do me a favour while I'm gone?'

'Absolutely. Anything,' she replied, shoe sizes promptly forgotten. She'd do anything she could to repay his kindness and make sure he didn't kick her off his boat. 'What do you need done?'

'I want the names of five charities to donate a thousand pounds to.'

Five thousand pounds was how much she was paying him to keep her hidden onboard *Camelot*. She swallowed. 'You're donating five thousand pounds to charity?'

He remained silent.

She forced herself to ask a different question. 'The search parameters...?'

He shrugged and her mouth went dry. His shoulders were *the best*. She could imagine dancing her hands across them, glorying in their breadth, testing their strength...watching his eyes darken with desire as she did so. A bit like they were doing now...

Fingers clicking under her nose had her blinking. 'Earth to Cleo!'

She jerked and blinked. 'Sorry! Off with the fairies.' Heat flooded her cheeks. 'Parameters...?' she croaked.

'Local would be preferable, and I'd like some proof of efficacy.'

'Consider it done.'

He turned and started up the steps. 'Same rules as before—keep the door locked, don't answer if anyone knocks and...' He held a finger to his lips.

'I'll be as quiet as a church mouse,' she promised.

'No dancing,' he said with a grin, closing the door behind him.

She stared at that closed door, feeling oddly bereft. Jude might not be chatty, but his presence was oddly reassuring. Shaking herself, she pulled out her phone and started researching local charities. What on earth would he be into, though? What would he like to support—be *proud* to support? Where on earth should she start?

Abandoning her phone, she reached for pen and paper and jotted down all the things she knew about Jude. He was a writer. He lived on a narrow boat. She tapped the pen against her chin. He'd been in London to attend his grandmother's funeral. He'd lost his brother in a car accident nine months ago. No wonder he rarely smiled. She couldn't begin to imagine how awful it would be to lose Margot like that, so suddenly.

What on earth...? Losing Margot in *any* fashion would completely and utterly gut her. Her chest clenched and her breathing grew rapid. If she didn't succeed in lying low for the next fortnight...

'Stop it!' she hissed, forcing herself to take

deep breaths, releasing them in slow, controlled measures as her therapist had taught her. She needed to stop imagining worst-case scenarios. It wouldn't do anyone any good. She needed to conserve her energy for keeping her promise to Margot and not being too much of a nuisance to Jude.

She stared at her list. Seizing the Jason Diamond book, she read Jasper's bio and added 'cricket lover' to the list. Pulling her phone towards her, she started madly searching the Internet, losing herself in the research. She made lists of lists, eventually narrowing the selected charities down to five local—or at least local-ish—options for him.

She froze when someone jumped onto the stern deck and went cold all over. Was someone going to knock, try to break in?

The door opened...

And Jude appeared. Sagging, she glanced at her phone to find an hour and twenty minutes had passed in a flash, just like that.

His brows rose. 'Expecting someone else?'

'What?' She blinked. 'No! I've only just finished coming up with your five charities and I...'

'You?'

She surreptitiously covered the notepad with her hand. 'I got caught up in the research and hadn't realised so much time had passed.' She sent him a weak smile. 'For a moment there, I thought I might have to fight off a robber.'

He stared at where her hand rested on the pad and her stomach scrunched up tight. She nodded at the bags he held, hoping to distract him. 'What have you got there?'

When his attention turned to the bags, she pulled the pad onto her lap and pushed it down between the dinette seat and the wall.

'One pair of running shoes, size four.'

He set them on the seat beside her. She stared at them and then at him. He couldn't mean…? 'I can't go running with you, Jude.'

'Sure you can.'

'If someone recognises me…' She rubbed her hands over her face. It'd be an absolute disaster. 'I can't risk it. I…'

'And in this bag are two wigs. Now, I know they'll probably itch, but it's better than you staying on board and climbing walls.'

She bit her lip. To be able to go for a run… But if she was seen… If she was seen *with a man* it'd be splashed across the front pages in an instant: *Cleo the serial dater*. And what if the press then dug deeper to find out who Jude was? What if they discovered he was Jasper Ballimore? He'd be unmasked. The scandal would explode! Margot would be devastated. And Cleo would've let everyone down—*again*.

'Cleo!'

She snapped to at the command in Jude's voice. 'Try the wigs on.'

He'd gone to so much trouble. The least she could do was try on the wigs. *Model passenger, remember?* She pulled the first box towards her and lifted the lid. Oh, wow. These were proper wigs, not cheap knock-offs bought for fancy dress. The first one was honey-blonde with long plaits and a fringe. She couldn't help grinning. 'Did you also get me denim overalls and a piece of straw to chew?'

Maybe Jude had a cowgirl fantasy. And maybe that would be kind of fun...

*Gah! Stop it.*

'The other one is, in my opinion, the real *pièce de résistance.*'

He uttered the phrase with the most deliciously perfect French accent and leaned back against the kitchen bench, the picture of relaxed ease, but she sensed an alertness, or perhaps an anticipation, in him that piqued her curiosity.

Pulling the second box towards her, she lifted the lid and her eyes went wide. The wig was a riot of light-brown curls that would hang down past her shoulders. She ran a light finger over a curl. 'This is really lovely.'

'The sales lady said you'd need to be careful with it if you wanted to maintain the curls, but nobody in real life has hair that perfect unless they've just come from the hairdresser. Messing it up would make the disguise all the more perfect.'

He reached out as if to do exactly that, but she held it out of reach. 'Let me try it on first. Then we can mess it up.' Racing into the bathroom, she tried it on and stared at her reflection. *Oh, wow.*

'Well?' Jude called out.

She moved back into the main cabin. Jude's jaw dropped. 'I wouldn't think you the same woman.'

His gaze travelled over her face in a way that had her nerves pulling tight and a pulse at her throat thrashing. Her breath caught as an expression akin to hunger stretched through his eyes, but then his lips thinned and he shook his head.

'It's all wrong with what you're wearing. This—' he gestured to her new mane of hair '—is too perfect, too formal. While this—' he gestured to the rest of her '—is casual and…'

*And* what?

'It doesn't work together.'

She wanted the floor to open up and swallow her. The only way Jude had been looking at her was as a problem he needed to fix. He wasn't looking at her as a woman he found attractive. She didn't *want* him looking at her that way either!

Lifting her chin and pasting on a smile, she said, 'That's easily fixed. Do you have an elastic band?'

Turning, he searched in a drawer and handed her one.

She gestured to the beanie sitting on the bench. 'And that.'

He handed it to her.

She tied the wig into a low pony tail and jammed the beanie onto her head.

He cocked his head to the side. 'With all of that hair pulled back, we can see more of your face now.'

Meaning someone might recognise her.

'You have another elastic band?'

He handed her a second one.

She shook out the wig and ran her fingers through the curls to frizz them up a bit, before fashioning the hair into two low bunches, pulling out wisps of hair to frame her face. 'How's that?'

He nodded slowly. 'That could work.'

His expression, though, told her that it was still a little too perfect. 'Wait until I do this.' Pulling the bands free, she grabbed his hairbrush from the bathroom and reefed it through the wig. When she was done, she held it out at arm's length. 'Now it's suitably frizzy.'

Without a word he handed her the blonde plaits. She pulled it on, the fringe tickling her forehead. He didn't say anything. Her hands went to her hips. 'Well?'

'I wouldn't have known it was you,' he finally

said. He pointed at the fringe. 'It changes the shape of your face.'

Moving back to stare in the bathroom mirror, she frowned. 'Fringes don't do me any favours. Which, in this instance, is perfect. With a bucket hat and sunnies, no one will recognise me.' Even Margot would be hard pressed to recognise her in this wig.

'Except you can't run in hat and sunnies—not at night.'

She pulled off the wig. 'I'm not running with you, Jude. I can't risk it.'

'You're going stir crazy.'

*Oh, God.* 'Have I been bothering you?'

He rolled his shoulders. 'No.'

*That clearly was a lie.*

'The thing is—' he rubbed a hand over his hair '—you're going to have to sign for your laptop tomorrow. I should've told you to address the package to me. I don't suppose you did, by any chance?'

Her stomach plummeted. She shook her head.

'But with a wig, a pair of sunnies and a beaten-up bucket hat…' Rifling in a top cupboard, he turned and tossed her a navy number. 'No one will recognise you.'

What if he was wrong?

'Same with the jogging, even without hat and sunglasses. Plus, there won't be many people about, not at this time of year. The canal path is lit, but the light is dim. And you'll be jogging behind me.'

To get out and expend some pent-up energy would be heaven.

'And I don't want you getting sick on my boat. Nor can I imagine Margot being thrilled if you turn up on the day of her wedding looking like a ghost.'

She shifted her weight from one foot to the other.

'We'll have an early dinner, give it time to settle and then go running when most people are already tucked up inside.'

He made it sound easy. He made it sound doable. Ever since she'd screwed up three years ago, exercise had been her crutch. It had helped her deal with *everything*. It gave her the resources to cope.

'The fresh air will do you good.'

Hadn't she told herself earlier not to keep imagining worst-case scenarios? Jude wouldn't lie to her. 'Okay.' She gave a short nod. 'In that case, I guess I should get dinner on now.'

He moved aside to let her slide out of the dinette and then slid in to where she'd been sitting while she gathered up the wigs and shoes and dumped them on her bed. Returning to the galley, she began pulling ingredients from the fridge.

'Cleo?'

'Hmm…?'

'What's this?'

Something in his tone had her swinging round. He sat with his back to her. Between his fingers he held up the list she'd made. She froze: the list of the things she knew about him.

Something had gone cold inside him. He turned and whatever she saw in his face had her paling.

'Are you keeping some kind of a dossier on me?' Had she figured out *who* he was? Beyond Jasper Ballimore, that was.

Giving a nod that held a world of fate, she set the red pepper she was holding on the bench and pressed her hands together. 'Turn the page over and read it…and the one after as well.'

Turning his back to her, he did as she said. He closed his eyes as he joined the dots.

'I wrote down what I knew about you so I could…'

'Choose five charities…' That would have a connection to him.

'That you'd be happy and proud to support.'

He'd set her the mission, wanting to give her something to do—to keep her occupied and stop her from surfing news sites, or constantly checking her phone, hoping to hear from Margot. If she didn't stop that soon, she'd drive herself batty.

'You startled me when you returned from your shopping trip. I'd become so wrapped up in the search I'd lost track of time. You were upon me before I realised. I didn't have a chance to get rid of my notes. I know it doesn't look good, but the motive was innocent.'

He nodded. Behind him, she started slicing and chopping. He ought to make conversation, move them on from this awkward moment, but he couldn't manage it. Not when the facts of his life were written in black and white in front of him, stated so baldly and starkly.

'So...' The strain in her voice made him wince. 'Do you approve of said charities?'

Pulling in a breath, he stared at the final list she'd compiled. It included a literacy programme for adults, home help for the elderly, the UK Canal Trust, a charity that paid for deprived local young people to learn to drive safely and a struggling cricket club. When was the last time anyone had taken this much trouble for him over such a simple task? Anyone else would've simply listed the things *they* thought worthy.

'Of course, those aren't the only things I know about you.' The sound of spitting oil and the scent of frying onions filled the air.

Why did the fact that she'd taken so much trouble touch him so deeply?

'That's the thing when you ask yourself a question like that, isn't it? Other answers bombard you for days afterwards.'

More hissing and spitting sounded. More delicious scents rose in the air.

'I know that you're kind to damsels in distress, which means you'd probably approve of a donation to a women's shelter.'

He added it to the list.

'You have a sense of humour—the joke knickers are proof of that.'

He didn't know whether to wince or laugh.

'So maybe a donation to a comedy festival? It's a good thing to do, to make people laugh.'

He jotted that down too, then held his breath as he waited to hear what else she thought she knew about him.

'You're ridiculously reclusive, but I don't think there's a hermits' association you can donate to— though maybe funding a writers' retreat would suffice. Peace and quiet for writers is something you'd approve of.'

*Absolutely.*

'Also, you can't cook, so donating to some kind of life skills programme might also be a worthwhile pursuit.'

Her observations were disconcertingly perceptive.

'And you understand the importance of exercise,' she finished. 'So in all likelihood an exercise education programme would appeal to you too.'

He stared at the fourth item on her list again. Sliding out from the dinette, he moved to the other bench so he was facing her. 'Matt was a good driver.' He didn't want her thinking Matt hadn't been a a good driver. Or a good person.

She met his gaze and nodded once, before turning back to the stir-fry, wielding her wooden spoon like a wand. 'I'm sorry you lost your brother, Jude. I can't even begin to imagine.'

Her quiet sympathy, its sincerity, lodged in his throat, making it impossible to speak.

'And I'm sorry that it was stated there on my list like that. As if…'

He raised an eyebrow, doing his best to look unmoved.

'As if it wasn't the biggest and worst thing that's ever happened to you.'

The edges of the room blurred. *The biggest and worst thing.* That summed it up exactly. A laugh scraped out of him. 'Want to hear the crazy thing? I was in the car when it happened, and basically walked away without a scratch. How wrong is that?'

He'd walked away while Matt…

Dead—in a split second—from hitting his head the wrong way. The world had gone dark after that night. The light had never come back.

Warm hands sliding into his brought him back to the present. He stared into eyes tempered with concern. 'What happened, Jude?'

He lifted a shoulder and let it drop. 'A deer. It raced out of the woods and onto the road.' He answered because he didn't know what else to do;

he didn't want to lose the comfort of her touch. 'Matt swerved to avoid it.'

Her lips parted and a sigh escaped, low and sympathetic.

'We'd been at the pub.' It had been Matt's turn to drive. 'I was the one who called time.' His heart gave a sick kick. 'I thought he was drinking low-alcohol beer.'

She swallowed. 'He was over the limit?'

'Only just. If I'd waited half an hour longer…'

Her hands tightened in his. 'It wasn't your fault.'

Forget waiting half an hour; ten minutes, two minutes, would've made all the difference. Even sixty seconds! Then they'd have avoided that deer. And Matt wouldn't have ploughed the driver's side of the car into a giant oak.

He flinched as that moment played through his mind. If only he'd known Matt had been drinking full-strength beer. If only…

'It wasn't your fault, Jude.' Cleo shook his hands and leaned closer. 'It wasn't!'

*Tell Elodie that.*

He slid his hands from hers. He didn't deserve her comfort. 'He left behind a grieving widow and a three-year-old son.'

She rubbed a hand across her chest, as if trying to ease an ache there. 'Such a terrible tragedy.'

A tragedy he should've prevented.

'Jude…'

'Enough, Cleo. You asked what happened and I told you.' Realising how brutal that sounded, he added, 'But I thank you for your condolences.'

She bit her lips, her eyes throbbing into his.

'I just don't have the heart to keep going over it.'

With a nod, she rose and went back to their dinner. A short time later, she set a plate of chicken stir-fry and rice in front of him. Considering the subject they'd been discussing, he shouldn't have had an appetite, but the sight of the food—colourful and glistening—and the scented steam that lifted into his face had him ravenous.

He forked food into his mouth and closed his eyes to savour it. 'I wish I'd lied to the coroner.' The words left him unbidden, making him blink.

She acted as if his confession was wholly normal, spearing a piece of broccoli on her fork, popping it into her mouth and chewing thoughtfully. 'Which bit would you lie about?'

He tried to eat slowly, but the food was insanely good. 'The bit where I said he lied to me about what he was drinking.'

'I'd lie to keep Margot out of trouble. I'd help her hide a body.'

He huffed out a laugh. Her lack of judgement was unexpected, and unexpectedly welcome. It eased some tightness inside him.

'Keeping schtum about that wouldn't have changed a thing.' His fingers tightened around his cutlery. 'All it's done is mar everyone's memory of Matt.'

'Nonsense!' Chicken and rice slid off her fork to splat back to her plate. 'Is that your enduring memory of your brother?' She pointed her fork at him and proceeded to answer her own question. 'Of course it isn't. You think of the time you were both at the crease in a county cricket match and won the day on the last ball of the final over.'

That had never happened, but he'd once fed Matt a perfect pass in a football game. Matt had drilled the ball into the top-left corner of the net for a stunner of a goal. It had been a thing of beauty.

'And the day you were his best man at his wedding.'

His lips twitched. He'd never seen Matt so nervous; he would never forget the look on his face when Elodie had appeared at the end of the aisle.

'And your grandmother would've remembered the day he graduated from university and…the time he burned down the back shed.'

Ha! That had actually happened.

'And his wife will remember the first time she met him and setting up house with him and the birth of your nephew.'

His chest clenched. To her dying day, Elodie would hold him responsible for Matt's death.

*'You should've known he was drinking. You knew how much stress he was under at work.*

*You should've taken on some of the responsibility. You should've been helping him.'*

She was right on every count—he should've.

He pushed his plate away.

Cleo pushed it back. 'You'll offend me if you don't finish it.'

He glared. She shrugged. 'You want to know why I'm such a Jasper Ballimore fan?'

*No. Yes.*

'Why?'

She scooped up more of the deliciousness on her plate and ate it, chewing slowly, as if savouring it. He picked up his fork with a scowl. The food was too good to waste, damn it.

'Jason Diamond helped get me through the worst of my therapy. You, or rather your pseudonym, appeared on my radar after a particularly... rough session.' She wrinkled her nose. 'It's hideous, coming face to face with one's own failings.'

She could say that again.

'Anyway, there was a book my therapist suggested I read, so on my way home I dropped into the big book shop on Piccadilly. Your publicist was there and you had dialled in to talk with her about your latest book. I couldn't believe how many people had come to listen to you speak. I mean, it's not like you were there in person signing books.'

She spiked a piece of chicken with her fork,

followed by a slice of pepper, a bit of carrot and a broccoli floret. He doubted she'd fit it all in her mouth. Setting down her fork, she rested her chin on her hands and stared at him. 'You spoke about your inspiration for Jason Diamond—how you'd always loved writing, how hard it could be but how satisfying too. And I thought to myself, here's a person who's living life on their terms, forging ahead with their dreams. And a tiny voice inside me whispered, *if he can do it, so can you.*'

He stared.

'It felt like serendipity—a tough therapy session and then stumbling into your inspiring talk.'

Inspiring? *Him?*

'So I bought the book my therapist recommended and your book too. I alternated reading a chapter of my therapy book with chapters of Jason Diamond. I swear his adventures kept me sane.'

That made him laugh.

He slowly sobered. 'I didn't give you enough credit when we first met. But, other than New Year's Eve, you hadn't appeared in the papers for…'

'Eight months. When Davide orchestrated that scene at the premier of a new movie and prostrated himself at my feet on the red carpet.'

His lip curled. 'That's right. He cried, claimed you'd destroyed all his dreams, or some such nonsense.'

'All news to me. We'd already parted ways,

but I'd agreed to honour the public commitments we'd made. He did it for the publicity, to get his name in the papers.'

Men like Davide and Clay had preyed on Cleo, taking advantage of her kindness and good nature. And in return the world had pointed an accusatory finger and condemned her—himself included. She wasn't perfect—her terrible dating record proved that—but he'd written her off as a vapid starlet based on what? The media write-up? There was *so* much more to this woman. Cleo had hidden depths he suspected he'd barely scratched.

Not only that, she'd made significant changes to her life. She'd turned her back on the celebrity scene. Cleo wanted to move on; it was just the rest of the world wouldn't let her. She had, in fact, done an amazing job at turning her life around, at no longer being the 'wild child'. She ought to be proud of herself. Her *family* ought to be proud of her.

'I just wanted you to know I'll always feel grateful to you for Jason Diamond and his kick-ass attitude.'

She pushed her plate away. As she'd finished most of her food, he asked, 'You done?'

At her nod, he seized his fork and polished it off. The brightening of her eyes was his reward. 'Seriously good,' he told her, sitting back and patting his stomach. 'And, for the record, I think you've done a great job at turning your life around. I expect Margot recognises that too. We're not going to let anything ruin that, I promise.'

It was a rash promise. But all this woman wanted to do was to save her relationship with her sister. She deserved the opportunity to do that.

Rising, he took their plates to the sink. She followed and butted him away with her hip. 'I'll do the dishes.'

The heat from her hip burned against his thigh. He edged away, the scent of pears filling his nostrils. 'You don't have to wait on me.'

'But you're doing all of the boat driving and stuff. This is me pulling my weight where I can.'

He snorted. 'The difference is that you're paying me an absolute fortune to do "the boat driving and stuff".'

'Money which you're giving away.'

She pointed down towards his easy chair. 'Go and do your puzzles.'

'And then in an hour we're going for a run,' he reminded her.

Her eyes shadowed. Reaching out, he touched her cheek. 'It'll be fine, I promise.'

She moistened her lips and his gut clenched.

Her gaze fluttered to his lips. Her chest rose and fell… It'd be so easy to reach across and press his lips to hers. To…

They both snapped away at the same moment. She busied herself with the dishes. Rather than grab a tea towel as he'd planned to, he retreated to the other end of the cabin and hid behind the newspaper. Nothing was going to happen between him and Cleo. He wouldn't let it. He might not be a hero, but she was alone and vulnerable. And he refused to be her next big mistake.

# CHAPTER FIVE

'OH, MY GOD!'

Cleo clapped her hands and danced on the spot while Jude locked the door behind them. When he turned, she took a plait in each hand and twirled them, beaming up at him. He shook his head, but one side of his mouth hooked up.

'Not a single person recognised me!'

'There weren't enough people out there to recognise you.'

There'd been a dog walker and three other joggers, and no one had given her a second glance. She danced on the spot again.

Jude braced his hands on his knees, his chest rising and falling from the exertion of their run. She took the opportunity to admire the powerful lines of his body. He wasn't built like the musclebound cover model that graced the covers of his Jason Diamond books, but he was strong and lean without a spare ounce of flesh. And those shoulders…

He glanced up and froze at whatever he saw in

her face. He straightened slowly, his gaze pinning her to the spot. 'What?'

'Nothing.' The word squeaked out of her.

A dark brow rose. It made her heart hammer harder.

'It's just that this—' she pulled off the wig and beanie '—was inspired, and I so needed that run, and I feel so much better for it—euphoric, you know? And for a moment there I was tempted to hug you.' *And more.*

She gripped her hands in front of her. 'But that's not a good idea, because we're all sweaty, and hugging you wouldn't be a good idea anyway, because…' *Oh, God, shut up now, Cleo.* 'You know…' *Floor, open up and swallow me.* 'I don't want to send mixed messages or give you the wrong idea…'

Jude closed his eyes. His lips turned white. She zipped her mouth shut.

'I'm in no danger of getting the wrong idea.' Those eyes snapped open. 'I've no intention of…' His hands made vague gestures, filling in the blanks. 'But no hugging is an excellent rule.'

She straightened. A rule now, was it? 'I couldn't agree more.'

She glanced at the ceiling, the floor and the wall—everywhere but at him. 'D'you want the first shower?'

He gestured her towards the bathroom. 'Knock yourself out.'

She showered, dressed in her cute though far from sexy pyjamas, bustled back into the main cabin and set about making hot chocolate. 'All yours,' she shot over shoulder, barely looking at him, sucking herself in as he eased past. Setting two steaming mugs on the table, she slid onto one of the bench seats—the one that ensured her back would be to the bathroom and Jude's bedroom. She didn't want to risk even the briefest glimpse of him emerging from the shower in nothing more than a low-slung towel, his skin gleaming...

*Stop it.*

What was wrong with her? Did she mean to spend her life lurching from mistake to mistake? Two days ago, she'd had a boyfriend!

*Yeah, but he was a bad boyfriend.*

*Oh, right, so that means it's okay to immediately jump into bed with another man to soothe your hurt pride, for revenge sex?*

She sipped her hot chocolate, letting its warmth filter into her. She didn't want to be the kind of person who did that. Given the circumstances, jumping into bed with any man was a bad idea. Besides the fact the media would have a field day if they found out, she'd had enough therapy to recognise a negative pattern when it slapped her on the head. The short-term satisfaction of sleeping with Jude wouldn't outweigh the damage she'd be doing to herself.

Where men were concerned, she was a disas-

ter. She needed to work out why. And, once she'd
done that, she'd work out what to do about it.
If she'd been looking for love in all the wrong
places, then she needed to start looking for it in
the right places, or in different ways.

Besides, Jude wasn't interested in her like that.
And who could blame him? He craved the quiet
life. A woman like her—one who landed herself
on the front pages of the newspapers with remarkable regularity—had to be his worst nightmare.
And yet he *had* let her stay. Because he knew
what it was like to lose a brother and he didn't
want her losing her sister.

She picked up the notepad with the list of charities she'd collated. Behind his stern appearance
and reserve, Jude was a bit of a softy. He didn't
need to be messed with by the likes of her. Setting
the notepad back down, she pressed her hands together. She'd abide by his rules. She'd be the easi-
est and best of boat roomies. She'd prove to Jude,
her father and Margot—especially Margot—
that she wasn't a hot mess. She'd prove that they
could trust her. And maybe one day they'd even
be proud of her.

Jude appeared wearing an old pair of track-
suit bottoms and a baggy, long-sleeve T-shirt that
didn't plaster itself against his body like a second
skin. Not that she'd have noticed if it had.

She gestured. 'I made you a hot chocolate. You

don't have to drink it if you don't want, but as I was making one for myself...'

Eyeing the mug as if it might bite him, he lifted it and took a sip. His brows shot up and something in his face lightened. 'This is good.'

She stuck her nose in the air. 'I'm an excellent hot-chocolate maker.'

It earned her a chuckle that made her breathe a little easier.

'You're also an excellent runner.'

He leaned against the bench; he *didn't* take the seat opposite, where their knees and feet might accidentally touch. She wished she hadn't mentioned hugging earlier. This was his boat, *his home*. He should be able to relax here. She needed to make things comfortable again.

'You'll find I'm excellent at many things.' That earned her one of those rare half-smiles. 'Therapy taught me the benefits of positive self-talk.'

'I think we can safely tick that KPI off the list for the day.'

She laughed. He could be funny when he wasn't concentrating on frowning all over the place. 'Running keeps me on an even keel—gives me an outlet for my excess energy, and the exercise endorphins are good for my brain. It's my number one strategy for staying on the straight and narrow.'

He crossed his legs at the ankles and stared at her over the rim of his mug, his eyes gratifyingly going glassy as he took another sip. 'You keep yourself on a tight leash.'

She didn't want to spiral out of control again. 'Thank you for making tonight possible, Jude. To be able to run is… It's everything.'

'I know.'

Something told her he understood exactly. What demons was Jude wrestling with? Did he really hold himself responsible for his brother's death?

She shook the thought away. It was none of her business. It didn't take a rocket scientist to see that Jude Blackwood was a private man—a *very* private man.

He took another sip of his drink and a low hum sounded from his throat. It vibrated through her in an utterly delicious way. 'How long since you had a hot chocolate?'

'I honestly can't remember. If you'd asked me, I'd have said not to bother making me one.'

'And look what you'd have missed.'

'And look what I'd have missed,' he echoed, his gaze stilling as it rested on her…darkening when it lowered to her lips. Two beats passed. He jerked upright and reached for the list of charities.

Cleo tried to catch her breath, trying to calm the crazy racing of her pulse. The way he'd looked at her… No, no, he wasn't interested in her *that* way.

He slid into the seat opposite, careful to angle

his knees away from hers. 'Which charity should I donate to first?'

'I'd start at the top and work my way down.'

'The literacy programme it is.' Pulling out his phone, his fingers flew over the screen. 'There, done.' He set it down again.

'What's the deal with that?' She nodded at the list. 'Why not choose your favourite from the list and give all the money to that one?'

He immediately removed his gaze from hers, and she wished she could retract the question. She was supposed to make things easy and light, be an undemanding travelling companion, not some nosy parker.

She opened her mouth to change the topic, but he spoke first. 'One of the last things my grandmother asked of me—made me promise—was, for the next year, to do one good thing every day.'

She stared at him. Her heart started to pound.

'And I reckon giving a thousand pounds to a worthy charity is a good thing to do. So, for the next five days, that's what I'm going to do.'

Her eyes burned. *Oh, Jude.* That would not have been what his grandmother meant; she was certain of it. He'd taken his grandmother's words entirely the wrong way.

A new thought slammed into her. *Oh.* Clasping her hands in her lap, she fought against the sudden burn of tears. 'That's why you let me stay.'

He hesitated, then shrugged. 'You needed help.

You asked for help. And it's not like you were interrupting me doing anything important. Having a passenger might be inconvenient, but not unworkable.'

*There you have it, Cleo: you're an inconvenience. Let that be lesson to you.*

In her lap, her hands gripped each other so hard they started to ache. She was simply part of a to-do list he needed to tick off.

*What were you hoping for?*

She fought the urge to rest her head on folded arms. 'You hid me, you agreed to let me stay, you bought me the essentials and today you made it possible for me to go for a run. *And* for the next five days you're giving a thousand pounds to charity.' As she named each event, she flipped out another finger. 'Are you trying to get ahead or are you simply a high achiever?'

He scowled at the contents in his mug. 'I broke my promise. Between my grandmother's death and her funeral—five days—I did *nothing* good.'

'You were grieving. Your grandmother would've understood.'

'A promise is a promise.'

The haunted expression in his eyes caught at her. 'Jude…'

He stood abruptly. 'Thanks for the hot chocolate. Crossword and whisky time.'

She watched him settle in his chair by the wood burner, her heart aching, burning and bleeding a little. But she kept her mouth zipped tight. Every instinct she had told her he wouldn't welcome her opinion.

*You're a smart and resourceful woman. Find a way to show him instead.*

Smart and resourceful women didn't have their photos snapped throwing punches at their boyfriends. Smart and resourceful women didn't let their sisters down.

Swallowing, she seized her Jason Diamond book and lost herself in a comforting world of heroics, where right and wrong were easy to identify; where injustices were righted and the good guys always prevailed.

Cleo strode into the main cabin and lifted her hands. 'What do you think?'

Jude stared at her for several long *fraught* moments. Finally, he nodded. 'If I were a photographer on the lookout for Cleo Milne, I wouldn't glance at you twice.'

She let out a breath. She had on the curly wig, which after her ministrations now sported a realistic and somewhat unattractive amount of frizz. She wore yoga pants, a sweatshirt and had twined an old scarf of Jude's around her throat. Grabbing the new sunglasses, she perched them on her nose. It was a far cry from her usual attire of jeans and wool blazer.

'We are just nipping out to get the laptop and

coming straight back?' she checked, trying to stop the panic from choking her.

He nodded.

Going out in the broad light of day was a far cry from jogging the canal path at night. She'd felt safe last night, with the darkness hiding her and Jude's back shielding her. But this felt risky.

He settled his hands on her shoulders. 'No one is expecting to find you in Berkhamsted.'

'There's plenty of speculation in the papers about where I could be, though. It's like a game of *Where's Wally?* Any journalist worth their salt will be keeping their eyes peeled.'

'You spend too much time on those damn news sites.'

He gave her shoulders a gentle squeeze. It put the heart back into her, and had her straightening her spine.

'You worry too much.'

True on both counts. But as soon as she had her laptop she could get back to work and stop fretting so much.

'Okay, let's do this.'

Standing on the towpath moments later, she tried not to fidget, but her stomach clenched so tight it almost cramped. Jude turned from locking *Camelot*'s door and frowned.

'Tell me a story.' The words blurted from her.

'A story?'

She nodded, keeping her gaze on the ground in

case anyone should be around… lying in wait and watching for her. Her pulse sky-rocketed. 'God, Jude, please take my mind off impending disasters.'

He stepped onto the path beside her and she nudged him. 'You're a master storyteller. I had to force myself to put your book down last night and get some sleep. It's the second time I've read this book. I know what happens, yet it's still so compelling. So *once upon a time…*'

A hollow laugh sounded through Jude. A master storyteller? Not likely. A master storyteller could pick up a pen or drag a keyboard towards them and words would pour from their fingertips. A master storyteller could lose themselves in a story for hours at a time, could wrestle with a plot problem for days and then feel ridiculously victorious when they found the answer.

None of this applied to him, not any more. Where once there'd been creativity and an intriguing swirl of ideas, a burning fire to pick up a pen, there was now a black hole. He might not have been physically injured the night of the accident that had claimed Matt's life, but he hadn't been able to write since.

At first he'd thought it a symptom of his grief. After Elodie had made it clear how bitterly she held Jude responsible for Matt's death, though, guilt had stifled all inspiration and had laid a rotting blanket over the first tentative buds of his reawakening creativity. He'd found himself utterly incapable of writing a story of honour and courage for an upright hero like Jason Diamond.

He now doubted he'd ever write again. Despair threatened to descend in a smothering black cloud. The thought of never again experiencing the rush and joy, the challenges and frustrations, of writing a story… To have that door now barred against him…

What right did he have to such consolation, though? If he hadn't been so selfish, he'd have noticed how much pressure Matt was under. He'd have noticed that Matt had started to drink more. He'd have noticed *something*. Then he could've done something to help. But he hadn't noticed anything. He hadn't *done* anything, too engrossed with his own selfish needs and wants.

And the worst of it was that he wondered now if it was because he hadn't *wanted* to notice anything, hadn't wanted to be dragged into working for his family's firm, Giroux Holdings. Because he'd wanted to lead the life *he'd* wanted.

And now it was too late, all too late. And Cleo wanted him to tell her a story? He knew she was nervous. He knew she sought distraction. He knew she had no idea what she asked of him but…

'Did you always know you wanted to write thrillers with a good guy hero?'

He forced himself to focus on the question rather than the chaotic blast of emotions roiling through him. He mightn't manage a story, but he could probably answer the odd question or two. 'In the early days, I had no idea what I wanted to write.' He frowned. 'Actually, that isn't exactly true. I wrote whatever took my fancy, no rhyme or reason. I must have at least a dozen manuscripts that aren't JD books in various stages of completion—from entire first drafts to just a few opening pages.'

'A dozen!' She halted to stare up at him, her eyes wide, as if she thought a dozen a particularly amazing number. Despite everything, he found himself fighting a smile. Maybe it was her wide-eyed awe, maybe it was the hair that fizzed around her face, completely messing with her normal tidy lines…. Those eyes, though, were the same compelling green. And those lips…

With an effort, he dragged his gaze from her lips and forced his legs forward again, only slowing his pace when he realised she had to rush to keep up. 'And, if we counted actual ideas for books, we'd be talking three or four times that number.' Talking about writing was much safer than focussing on his reactions to this woman.

She heaved a sigh as if his words had evoked the happiest of thoughts. He worked hard at keeping his gaze on the path in front of them.

'What kind of trees are those?' She pointed to the tall stand of trees bordering the towpath.

'Beech—very common. Harder to tell with no leaves on them, though.'

She made a noise in the back of her throat. 'I'm terrible at anything botanical. I've never had a garden. But it'd be lovely to have one.'

It seemed a small enough wish, and an achievable one. 'You'd need a big garden for those.'

'But don't they look pretty? Actually, not so much pretty as grand.'

She turned, hands on hips, to stare back the way they'd come, and he realised someone was coming along the path towards them. *Right...* 'Your name for the rest of the day is Fran.'

Her lips twitched, but she didn't look away from the beech trees. 'Look at the way the light is filtering through the branches. It'd make a really nice image.'

'For what?'

Pulling out her phone, she snapped a couple of pictures. 'In my spare time, I muck around with creating website headers. Much like you do with story ideas.'

*Did*, not *do*. *Past tense*.

But he tried to see what she saw in the beeches, tried to see what had captured her imagination. 'It's…peaceful.' His shoulders loosened a fraction. 'A little bleak, but kind of timeless.'

She smiled up at him, as if he'd given her the

right answer. Turning, she started walking again, mumbling a greeting to the couple as they passed, but keeping her gaze lowered.

'So, back to our conversation…'

*What conversation?*

'If you hadn't written the JD books—or if they hadn't been picked up by a publisher—which of your many projects would you have pursued instead?'

Her knuckles had turned white where her hand gripped the strap of her handbag. The couple hadn't recognised them—had barely looked at them—but her fear of being unmasked overrode what logic should have told her. If he couldn't find a way to help her relax, her tension would give the game away. So he told her what he hadn't told anyone. 'A young adult fantasy trilogy.'

Her hand abruptly unclenched. 'Like *Lord of the Rings*?'

*Lord of the Rings* was one of his favourite books. Did she like it too?

'It takes place in a kingdom called Ostana. No elves or orcs, but there are dragons and—'

'Are the dragons good or evil?'

'Generally good, but they're like people, in that they can be a bit of both.'

'Tell me more.'

'There's a mysterious dark force threatening the world, a boy who doesn't know he's a king, and a girl who doesn't realise she's a dragon rider.'

She did a funny little skip and clapped her hands. 'Tell me they fall in love.'

'Yep.'

'And that together they save the world.'

'Ah, but it's not that simple, is it?'

He led the way off the towpath and into the town of Berkhamsted. It was eleven-thirty, and the town was bustling. From the corner of his eye he saw Cleo swallow. 'Eventually they save the world, but there are a lot of ups and downs first.'

'Tell me more!'

'Well, he's timid and runs away at the smallest sign of danger, while she's too cynical to believe in happy-ever-afters. Plus, she's bossy. They hate each other on sight.'

'Of course they do. But fate forces them together?'

He couldn't *not* smile. Her eyes had lost their hunted expression, replaced instead with the avid interest of a true reader. 'Something like that.'

'Tell me this trilogy is written.'

Was she actually holding her breath? 'Books one and two are. The third has been started.'

'Tell me I can read it.'

'And here we are at the delivery place,' he announced, pulling them to a halt.

She tensed. Her hand clutched the scarf she'd wound around her throat.

'*Look... Fran*, you're an actor. Think of this as a role.'

'Did you see me act?' she snapped. 'I was terrible.'

His head rocked back. 'No, you weren't. Your character was troubled, but you brought out her vulnerability beautifully. You made her sympathetic. She did some awful things, but the audience wanted her to find her happy-ever-after all the same.'

Her jaw dropped. 'You watched?'

He wasn't admitting anything. 'I caught a couple of episodes. And in today's drama series you're an ordinary person with slightly frizzy hair collecting a parcel. You need this particular parcel for an assignment because you're a mature student at the local community college.'

'What am I studying?'

'Horticulture.'

Her lips twitched. Her death grip on her scarf eased.

'I'll make a deal with you, Fran.'

Her lips twitched again.

'You do yoga, right?'

She nodded.

'If you relax your shoulders—ease them down from around your ears, unlock your jaw and unclench your hands—I'll let you read the first chapter of my trilogy this afternoon.'

She immediately did everything he asked. 'You *so* have yourself a deal… Brian.'

*Brian?* He nearly tripped up the first step.

Chuckling, she leapt up them lightly and reached the door before him. For the briefest of moments he wondered if he could write a similar scenario into one of his books. It could be fun at some stage during the third instalment of *The Crown and the Fire Wielder* if Clement and Ruby had to don disguises—Clement having to pull on a mantle of command while Ruby had to act meek and downtrodden.

Cleo opened the door and the thought slipped away as they waited together in line. It took a while for the assistant to locate Cleo's parcel and he snapped into hyper-vigilance mode.

*Like JD?* Ha! He was no hero. But he had no intention of letting anyone blow Cleo's cover.

Eventually the parcel was located, signed for and handed over. Keeping his steps steady, he moved towards the exit and gestured for Cleo to precede him through the door.

Except she grabbed his arm and tugged him to the side; maps of the local area were lined up in neat rows in front of them. The pulse in her throat raced. 'Impending disaster!'

What the hell?

'Across the road. The man in the blue jeans and grey woollen jumper...'

'Journo?'

'Yes.'

Glancing towards the counter, his jaw clenched. The assistant stared at them, her phone to her ear.

Cleo followed his gaze and swore softly. They'd been rumbled. And they needed to move fast.

Seizing Cleo's hand, he tugged her to the side door, shot out of it and set off down the street and into the bustling heart of the town. A shout sounded behind them and they broke into a run. Rounding a corner, he pulled her inside a huge discount fashion store, ones with racks of clothes everywhere.

Cleo took the lead and towed him to the back of the shop. They half-crouched when the journalist halted in front of the plate-glass window, ducking down when he turned to peer in their direction. Keeping low, Cleo led him to the fitting rooms. She collapsed onto a bench seat. He locked the door behind them and gestured for her to lift her feet onto the bench—in case anyone happened to look beneath the door.

Maybe he'd grown used to narrowboat living, but the room didn't feel too cramped. What he wouldn't give to be safely tucked away on *Camelot* right now, feeling cramped and unable to escape the mouth-watering scent of pears.

'What are we going to do?' she whispered. 'That witch of a sales assistant will have given him our descriptions. And he knows what we're wearing.'

Setting his backpack on the bench beside her, he rummaged round, emerging triumphantly with her blonde wig.

Her jaw dropped. 'You wonderful man!'

She immediately pulled off the frizzy wig and donned the plaits. The difference it made was remarkable.

'Here, put this on.'

He blinked when she shoved the curly wig at him.

'Hurry up.' She pulled the backpack towards her to check its contents. Grinning, she pulled out a battered beanie he'd forgotten was in there. 'Truly wonderful,' she murmured, pointing at him.

He didn't tell her the beanie was an oversight. It had been ages since anyone had thought he'd done anything wonderful. He pulled on the wig. He looked ridiculous, but she pulled a hair-tie from her handbag, gestured for him to turn around and made some kind of low bun at his nape. The touch of her fingers had hard darts of electricity zapping across his scalp. He had to clench his teeth and silently recite his eight-times table.

Once she was done, she pulled the beanie over the wig until it covered his ears, curls spilling out to frame his face. He blinked at his reflection. He no longer looked like a man wearing a woman's wig. He looked like a hippy…and that could work.

'D'you have a shirt on under your jumper?'

He pulled the jumper over his head, careful not to disturb her handiwork. She stowed the jumper in the backpack. 'I hate to ask you…'

He was already ahead of her. 'I'll go out there and get you a completely different outfit.'

'Then I'll do the same for you.'

He came back with oversized denim overalls, a multi-striped jumper in some kind of fuzzy fabric and chunky, dangly earrings. She grinned when she saw the ensemble. Taking the backpack, he moved to the dressing room next door. A few minutes later, she tapped on the door. He took one look and gave her a thumbs-up.

She blew out a breath. 'Okay, give me your sizes.'

He told her, taking her clothes to stow in the backpack. She returned with super-baggy black cargo pants, a tight long-sleeved T-shirt with a 'peace' sign emblazoned on the front...and a cardigan! He nearly snorted with laughter.

Her eyes danced as she pushed a big tote bag into his hands. 'That should be big enough to stow the backpack.' Which was when he noticed the wicker basket she held over one arm. *Perfect.*

'Give us a cover story,' she ordered.

'We're a couple who are into sustainable living. We have a stall at the local market where we sell handmade crafts, though we've both part-time jobs to help pay the rent. You work at a nursery while I'm a night-time shelf-stacker at a grocery store. And today we're...' he glanced at her wicker basket '...going on a picnic.'

Ten minutes later, they sauntered out of the

shop as two completely different people. Cleo stopped at a deli and bought a loaf of sourdough, cheese, bananas and a bottle of sparkling water. She took his arm and they made their way back to the boat, looking like a pair of young lovers.

Back onboard *Camelot*, he ushered her down the steps, pushed the door closed and slid the lock into place, before swinging to face her. She had to be frantic. She...

His mind blanked. She'd bent at the waist, both hands clapped over her mouth to stifle her laughter. 'Oh, my God, Jude. I should be beside myself, but that was so much fun.'

She said the words as if they ought to start with capital letters, so in his mind he gave them capitals: *So Much Fun*.

She was right. Which made no sense...

Her eyes danced and her lips curved upward, and it woke something deep inside him, shaking it free and making him glad to be alive. He could no more stop from leaning across and pressing his lips to hers then he could have stopped the tide.

# CHAPTER SIX

CLEO SMELLED LIKE pears and tasted like freedom.

And she froze, as if taken totally unawares.

*What the hell...?*

Jude started to move away, but her fingers tangled in the ridiculous cardigan he wore, dragging him back, her mouth opening under his...

And he was gone. Cupping her face in his hands, he devoured her, learning the shape of her mouth, learning what made her shiver or brought a low hum to life in the back of her throat. Every time she sighed, moaned and deepened the kiss something inside him loosened and unfurled, forming an entirely new shape where before there'd been nothing but a hard, dark lump. Desire, need and the invigorating thrum of blood coursed through his veins.

Curling her fingers into his cardigan all the more securely, as if anchoring herself there, she devoured him back and all thought fled as things fizzed and sparked with an urgency that ought to have shocked him—that might have shocked him if he'd been able to think straight.

Growling with hunger and heat, he tried to temper the inferno that gripped him, tried to temper his strength, afraid of holding her too tight. As if she had no such concerns, she lifted up on tiptoe and flung her arms around his neck. The full length of her body pressed against his.

He backed her up until they reached the table, lifted her onto it and settled between her thighs. He caught her soft cry inside his mouth and a rainbow of colour arced behind his eyelids as their bodies strained towards each other.

Her fingers dug into his buttocks as if to drag him nearer. His fingers dug into her hips as he pulled her as close to him as he could, air hissing between his teeth when small, seeking hands slid beneath his shirt to explore the contours of his stomach and chest, her palms grazing against his nipples and making him jerk.

It was too much too soon. He couldn't breathe.

Dragging his mouth from hers, he pulled in gulping breaths of much-needed air as they stared at each other, their chests rising and falling, air sawing in and out of their bodies.

Cleo couldn't pull her gaze from Jude's. The blue of his eyes was piercing and bright, and it sent a thrill circling through her.

How could a simple kiss be so *consuming*?

She touched fingers to her lips. It hadn't been simple, though, had it? That kiss had reverberated through her in a way a kiss never had before. His hands cupping her face had made her feel safe. They'd been gentle but strong—their strength had become her strength. And the kiss had sunk deep, the echoes of it imprinting onto muscle and bone. That had to mean something...

She blinked. It couldn't mean *anything*!

Planting her hand in the middle of his chest, she pushed him away, slid off the table and backed up a step. 'You said no hugging. It was a rule.'

She didn't recognise the voice that scraped out of her throat. She recognised the self-loathing that immediately smothered all the sparkling blue brightness in Jude's eyes, though.

*Oh, no, Jude. Don't do that to yourself.*

Kissing was a bad idea, but it didn't have to mean the end of the world. He shouldn't hate himself for it. Rather than focus on the confusion raging inside her, or the desire coiling through her, she focussed on finding a way to rid that expression from his eyes.

Sliding in at the dinette before her legs gave way, she dragged off her wig and slanted a smile in his direction. She couldn't let him take the blame for what had just happened. That wouldn't be fair. *She* was the train wreck, remember?

'However, as we didn't hug—not really—I

'But I'd appreciate it if you could hand me up a sandwich in half an hour.'

'Deal.'

Cleo spent the rest of the day working. Not on one of her many paid projects, but on an odd and sudden inspiration. Rather than stamp it out or ignore it, as had become her habit in recent years, she decided to indulge it. Because seven years of not having any real joy in her life...that was awful!

At seventeen, the acting out and partying had been an attempt to outrun the grief of losing her mother. It hadn't worked; therapy had helped her see that. But it now seemed she'd gone too far the other way, viewing fun, laughter and joy as things she ought to avoid.

She didn't want to live a joyless life. She could experience fun and gladness without descending into those old damaging patterns of behaviour. She needed to make room to let joy back in.

Late afternoon, Jude called down that they were docking in a marina and for her to stay out of sight.

*A marina? Why?* Was everything okay? Was there an issue with *Camelot*'s engine or...? *Oh.*

Her heart dropped to her feet. He wanted to be of her, didn't he? He was going to ask her to ve. Because of that kiss. And because they'd

guess we didn't technically break any rules. So that's okay.'

He backed up to his easy chair, reaching behind to swivel it round before collapsing into it—as if he didn't trust himself to sit at the table so close to her. He was probably worried she'd jump him and kiss him again.

Her fingernails dug into her palms. He might have a point. It was exactly what her body was demanding she do. Except...she wasn't that person any more.

*Don't ruin everything. Don't revert to type.*

She *needed* to be better. She swallowed. *He* deserved better. And she needed him to not feel bad about this or it'd be another item on the long list of things to feel guilty about.

Sending him the tiniest of smiles, she shrugged. 'It was a hell of a kiss, though.'

He rubbed his hands over his face. 'I'm sorry, Cleo. I...'

'Don't.' Her smile faded. 'I was as into that as you were.'

'But I promised to look after you.'

'No, you didn't!' Her every muscle stiffened. 'You promised to give me a place to hide— *nothing* more. Jeez, Louise, you just went above and beyond in helping keep my identity secret, and I'm *really* grateful for that. But it is *not* your job to look after me.'

Pursing his lips, he stared at her. 'Is that why you kissed me back—because you were grateful?'

Her laugh might've held an edge of hysteria. She did her best to rein it in. 'That was *not* a pity kiss, Jude.' *Nuh-uh.* 'That little adventure of ours, managing to avoid detection and giving that journalist the slip... I haven't felt...'

Resting elbows on his knees, he leaned towards her. 'What?'

'It made me feel more alive than I have in...' *Seven years.* 'In a long time.' She moistened her lips. 'It went to my head and I felt like...' She swallowed, clearing her throat. 'Celebrating.'

But that had been entirely the wrong way to celebrate. Though now she had to wonder if, in keeping herself on such a tight leash for the last few years, had she chased all joy from her life? She pushed the thought away to deal with later.

'Also.' She pinned him with a glare. 'I don't give you permission to look after me.'

He straightened.

'By all means help me out if, like today, my cover is threatened, but I *can* look after myself. That whole calling myself a damsel in distress was supposed to be a joke.'

Delicious frown lines deepened. Everything about this man was delicious. It was enough to make a grown woman weep.

'You're going through a lot at the moment, though, Cleo.'

'So are you.'

The frown became a scowl. 'You just broke up with your cheating boyfriend.'

She folded her arms. 'You just lost your grandmother.'

He paled and her heart went out to him. He'd been dealing with the weight of the world.

'In my world, losing grandmas trumps cheating boyfriends every single time.'

He blinked. Colour rushed back into his face.

She clapped a hand to her mouth. 'I'm sorry, that sounded so much better in my head than it did out loud.' This wasn't some kind of contest and she hadn't meant to make it sound like one. 'I'm sorry,' she repeated. 'Don't ever put that in the book. I don't think readers would like it.'

He laughed, as if he couldn't help it. It wasn't a particularly joyful laugh, but she'd take wha she could get. 'If you get to look after me. I g to look after you.'

Blue fire flashed from his eyes. 'I don't n looking after!'

She spread her hands, as if to say, 'I re case'. 'I'm starving. You want some lunc

He glanced at his watch and looked to h some kind of calculation in his head. ' set off ASAP.'

An excellent idea; she wanted to p distance between them and that rud ist as possible.

nearly been unmasked. Because she was a mess, and he didn't want a mess like her in his life.

And she couldn't blame him, because if he was seen with her it would lead to speculation, and speculation could unmask his secret identity. 'You look like you've lost your best friend,' Jude said, coming below deck. 'Everything okay?'

She made herself smile and nod. A marina made sense. Jude was a decent guy; he wasn't just going to dump her on the side of the canal. He'd find her passage on another boat first. *Then* he could wash his hands of her with a clear conscience.

She had a crazy urge to yell and throw things, stamp her feet and cry.

'Cleo?'

Jude didn't deserve a temper tantrum. She'd be a model passenger if it killed her. 'A marina? Is all well?'

He frowned. 'Do you trust me?'

She might only have known him for three days, but in that time he'd kept her secret, had kept her hidden and he hadn't betrayed her when it would've been in his financial interests to do so. She nodded. 'Yes.'

If he thought now was the right time to part company, she'd accept it with all the grace she could muster.

'Here's the thing... After the incident in

Berkhamsted, I think the media will start scouring the canals for you again.'

*Oh!* She should've thought of that. If that kiss hadn't completely befuddled her, maybe she would have.

*Don't think about the kiss.*

Letting out a slow breath, she straightened. 'D'you have a plan?' One that didn't include dumping her on someone else's narrow boat.

He opened his mouth then frowned. 'What smells so good?'

She gestured to the kitchen bench. 'Banana bread. I baked some earlier.' *For joy.* 'I found some flour. I didn't think you'd mind.'

'Of course I don't mind. I…' He shook himself. 'The plan…?'

He straightened. 'As long as you're in agreement, I thought of organising a car to get us as far away from here as possible.'

'*Excellent* plan.'

Her relief was due to the excellent plan and not the fact he didn't want to be rid of her. 'When?'

'We'll leave under the cover of darkness.'

*Jason Diamond style?* She grinned. 'You've always wanted to say that, haven't you?'

One corner of his mouth twitched, but then he sobered. 'I need to go out for a bit and make the arrangements. In the meantime…' he stalked into his bedroom and returned with the tote bag they'd bought earlier '…you'll need to pack.'

'Roger that.'

He headed for the door. 'Same drill.'

She nodded. 'Don't answer the door. Don't make any noise.'

'I'll be as quick as I can.'

Packing took no time at all. What else ought she do? They'd bought food for dinner. Was 'under the cover of darkness' before or after dinner? She paced for a while before pulling out her laptop and working on her fun project again to give her mind something different to focus on.

It was dark when Jude returned. 'A car will collect us at ten.'

That answered the dinner question. 'Where are we headed?' North was her guess—a remote farmhouse in Yorkshire or Northumberland would be perfect.

'Still being decided. Things are in motion, though. I'm just waiting to hear back.'

*From whom?* She didn't ask as he moved into his bedroom, presumably to pack his own things. And probably to avoid her. He'd barely looked her in the eye since that kiss.

They ate crumbed steak with mash and veg for dinner. She didn't pester him with questions about *the plan*. He seemed oddly keyed up, so she remained on her best model-passenger behaviour.

She also did her best not to notice the way his eyes half-closed on each mouthful, as if relishing every bite. It did strange things to her insides—made her stomach soften and her chest clench. It made her want to cook her entire repertoire of meals to discover his favourite.

He glanced up and caught her stare. 'What?'

She forced herself back to the mechanics of eating. 'Do you ever treat yourself to a pub lunch?' Wasn't that one of the things people did when cruising the canals—stop to enjoy the delights of a canal-side pub? Because Jude quite clearly enjoyed his food.

'Nope.'

'Why not?'

He didn't answer, just shrugged. Talk about excluding joy from one's life. He made her look like an amateur.

'I'll sometimes grab a pie from a village bakery.'

*That* was as much as he allowed himself? The admission had her wanting to cry.

Afterwards, they cleaned up and did the dishes. There was still nearly three hours before the car was due to collect them, though. And, while they didn't speak about it, now that night had fallen the memory of their kiss burned in all the spaces between them.

Jude retreated to his chair with the paper. She cut banana bread and made them hot chocolate, which they sipped in their individual corners. Her mind worked overtime. She waited until the contents in her mug had reached the halfway point before speaking. 'When I was in therapy, I had to keep a gratitude journal.'

He glanced up, watchful...silent.

'I scoffed at the time, thought it silly and gimmicky, but it really did help.'

He looked torn between saying something unfriendly such as, *So what?* or something supportive, such as *Good to hear.* In the end, he opted for silence—no surprises there.

'I think we should do that for as long as we're on this...adventure. I'll go first.'

The newspaper rustled in his lap. 'Why do *I* have to do it?'

Because it would help him focus on the positive things in his life. Because it would help him realise what his grandmother had meant. 'You don't. Not if you don't want to.'

His shoulders unhitched.

'But it would keep me company and make me feel less vulnerable and alone.'

Those glorious shoulders tensed again. 'I believe that's what they call emotional blackmail.'

She wrinkled her nose. 'I feel as if I've ruined your life.' His jaw dropped and she added, 'Not your whole life, just these couple of weeks where I'll be invading your privacy.'

'Cleo...'

'And knowing that there are some things in

your life every day that you feel happy about and grateful for would help ease my guilt.'

He set his mug and the newspaper onto the small table beside him. 'You're making banana bread and real food. You've nothing to feel guilty about.'

'Hey, I said I'd go first!'

She stared at him in mock exasperation and he huffed out a laugh. 'You're incorrigible, you know that?'

She stuck her nose in the air, but her insides had started a little tap dance. 'I've been called worse.'

He shook his head, gesturing for her to continue.

'Okay, so we need to name three things each. First on my list: I'm ridiculously grateful we managed to avoid detection in town this morning. And this is going to sound a bit twisted, but it was also fun—edge of your seat stuff, like watching your football team surge forward in the last seconds of extra time and scoring a goal just as the final whistle sounds.' She folded her hands on the table. 'Incredibly exhilarating...but I really don't want to go through it again.'

'Noted.' Jude had no intention of letting anything like that happen again. 'First on my list is the banana bread and dinner—both delicious.'

She pursed lips that were pure temptation.

The continuous effort to resist them left him exhausted. Leaving *Camelot*'s close confines would be a relief. His lips twisted; even if it did come with problems of its own.

'There are lots of things to feel grateful for, or that were good about my day, but there are two in particular—'

'Like what?' he cut in. Other than the amazing food she'd served up to him, he was struggling to think of anything else to put on his list.

She nibbled a corner of her banana bread. 'There are always the old chestnuts to fall back on—like, I have my health, my family have their health, I have somewhere safe to sleep, have food in my belly, clothes on my back, blah blah. And don't get me wrong; I *am* grateful for all of those things.'

He nodded. Not everyone was so fortunate.

'And there are more besides that might usually make my list—like our run last night. The air was crisp, it didn't rain, there weren't many people about and that stretch of the river was really pretty.'

It was why he'd stopped there.

'I'm glad I have my laptop, that I had a good night's sleep and that I made banana bread. That I'm no longer climbing the walls.'

She rattled them all off with such ease. He fought a scowl; it wasn't a contest.

'And I'm *really* glad my face wasn't plastered

on the front pages of any newspapers today,' she added with a roll of her eyes.

Her name had appeared, though. That 'where's Cleo?' version of *Where's Wally?* continued to create speculation. It had to be playing on her mind.

'But none of those things made it onto your list?'

'Nope.'

He tried to not sound grudging. 'What's your number two, then?'

'I had an epiphany.'

He shuffled up a little higher in his seat. 'Which was…?'

She cupped her hands around her mug, though he suspected her hot chocolate had been drunk long ago. 'Our adventure today…'

'Some people would call it a misadventure.'

'Meh…potato potahto. It ended well, so I think we can drop the *mis*.'

He acknowledged the hit and gestured for her to continue.

'Getting away with it gave me a weird high and I suddenly realised that whenever I feel like that—'

'Like what, exactly?'

'Excited, jumping up and down with… I don't know.' She chewed on her bottom lip. He did his best to not notice. 'Glee, laughter, a sense of fun, delight… I realised I try to stamp those things out, try not to feel them.'

He leaned towards her and fancied he could smell pears. 'Why the hell would you do that?'

She stared at her hands. 'The first four years after my mother died, I was trying to hide from what I was feeling—the grief. I felt lost and I tried to hide that beneath a veneer of fun and partying hard. We already know how that played out and how I've since tried to turn over a new leaf.'

He nodded.

'For the last three years, though, I've equated things like glee and flights of fancy and lots of laughter with losing control. I've been so focused on keeping on the straight and narrow—trying not to do anything that would horrify and disappoint Margot and my father—that, basically, I've been murdering all and any high emotion that's bubbled to the surface.'

She mimed the stabbing knife from the shower scene of *Psycho*, her eyes rueful but with a hint of laughter in their depths, and he couldn't entirely smother a laugh.

'I hadn't realised that until today. And it struck me as kind of dense.'

'Only kind of?' He raised an eyebrow.

She poked out her tongue. 'Anyway, I'm through with doing that. Your turn.'

Cleo had let herself fully indulge in a moment of stress-relieving laughter, had gloried in her close escape, had let herself be wild and free—and what had he done? He'd gone and kissed her.

'No, no!'

Her voice broke into his thoughts.

'You're not supposed to look like that when we're making our gratitude lists.'

'Like what?'

'Angry…scowly.'

'Can we list regrets?' The words growled from him.

'Absolutely not! This is a gratitude list—things to feel good about, not beat ourselves up for.' Her eyes narrowed. 'And, for the record, that kiss shouldn't be a regret.'

'It sure as hell didn't make your list of things to feel grateful for.'

'Only because I was being tactful,' she shot back.

He stabbed a finger on the arm of his chair. 'It shouldn't have happened.'

'Maybe not, but it was a damn fine kiss all the same. One I'm not going to forget in a hurry.' Her lips curved. 'I bet I'll still remember it when I'm eighty. And, when I do, I bet I happy-sigh.'

His stomach clenched; *everything* clenched. The kiss had been hell-on-wheels spectacular. It had blown him open, and to deny that he wanted to kiss her again would be a lie. But it didn't change the fact that it shouldn't have happened.

He shouldn't play with that kind of fire. He'd had his heart shredded by a woman once before.

He wasn't going to allow that to happen again. And even if Cleo was nothing like Nicole, his ex, she was still a hot mess. He had no desire whatsoever to be her next big mistake. He'd witnessed what loving and then losing his brother had done to Elodie. He wasn't going to open himself up to that kind of pain.

Cleo had boarded his boat and had promptly sworn off men. Given her situation, it was a smart move. He wouldn't mess that up for her.

'I refuse to regret something that has the potential to be a happy memory.' Cleo held her head high. 'It was just…a moment. We stopped when we should've, called a halt when we should've. It's only if I follow up on it now that it would become self-destructive. And we've already agreed we're not going to do that.'

Her words brought no comfort because he wanted to, with his every fibre. But by this time tomorrow she'd know exactly who he was and…

*No. Just…no.*

'I don't think you ought to regret it either. And if you do then I don't want to hear about it.'

Her candour, delivered with sledgehammer bluntness, startled a laugh from him.

She raised an eyebrow. 'Okay, what's your number two?'

'I saw an otter.'

Her eyes widened. 'When?'

'Just before we pulled into Berkhamsted this morning.'

'And you didn't call me? Why not?'

Because he'd thought she was trying to stay out of sight. 'It was there one moment and then it was gone. It all happened too quickly.'

Her face turned wistful and he nodded. 'It's one of the best things about cruising the canals— catching sight of a kingfisher or watching swans glide by. And, when I'm very lucky I occasionally see an otter. I saw a badger once.'

'What about hedgehogs?' She gave a gusty sigh. 'I love hedgehogs.'

'From time to time. They're endangered now.' His plan meant otters and hedgehogs wouldn't be featuring on the agenda for the foreseeable future, though. His stomach churned again at how close he'd come to blowing her cover. After promising to keep her safe, he'd almost handed her to the media on a platter! If they'd been caught...

But they hadn't been. He let out a slow breath. They were still safe. Soon, though, this section of the canal would be crawling with journalists. It was time to get her well and truly out of their reach. He should discuss the plan with her, except it'd change her focus from her epiphany to her fears. And, once she knew the truth, everything would change.

'What's third on your list?' he asked instead.

A slow smile spread across her lips.

*Don't focus on her mouth. Hmm, look— delicious banana bread, see?* He shoved the last bite into his mouth in an attempt to distract himself, but all it did was stick in his throat.

'I did a fun thing. A fun work thing—only it wasn't work because it wasn't an actual job. It was a bit of play—for joy, you know? I had a ball. Want to see?'

Before he could answer, she lifted her laptop from the spot on the seat beside her where it was charging and lifted the lid. Retrieving a file, she turned the computer to face him. His jaw dropped when he realised what was facing him: a website home page…for *him*.

His Jasper Ballimore author headshot was a cartoon of an archetypal musclebound hero, and she'd clearly grabbed it from his current website, as it sat to the left below a header. This header was all swirling black shadows and golden fire, which managed to look both threatening and beautiful at the same time. Rather than Jasper Ballimore, the name Jay Ballimore emerged in various shades of teal and sapphire from the shadow and flame.

'Jay Ballimore?' he murmured.

'I thought, if you were writing a young adult fantasy series, you'd need to write under a different name than the one you use for your thrillers.'

She scrolled down. There was a paragraph beside the author photo that he couldn't read from this distance, and beneath that she'd created three mock-up covers for the trilogy he'd told her about as they'd walked into Berkhamsted.

'I thought "Jay Ballimore" sounded suitably fantasy-ish. Not all your thriller readers will follow you here—' she tapped the screen '—or vice versa, but you will get some crossover readers who adore the way you write.'

Was she one of them? He shook off the thought and gestured to her computer, his mind a tumble of confusion. *'Why...?'* Why would she go to so much trouble? Why would she invest so much time in something that would never become a reality? Things inside him bucked at that thought, as if they hadn't given up hope of finishing the series. Which was odd, and not entirely welcome.

He rose. 'May I?'

At her nod, he took the laptop, retreated to his seat and read the paragraph beside his photo.

*Let Jay Ballimore take you into a world of stolen thrones, ancient fire magic, cursed swords and majestic dragons in this brand-new fantasy series where a pair of seventeen-year-olds, who hate each other on sight and on principle, need to learn to work together if they want to save all that they love from destruction.*

She made it sound like a done deal!

*Well...?* The inner voice sounded a lot like his agent's. He ignored it.

He glanced up and she shrugged. 'Like I said—it was fun. I love doodling around like this.'

Doodling? This wasn't doodling…

'And, while I love Jason Diamond, thrillers aren't my usual jam. Fantasies are, though. My fave authors are Naomi Novik, Tolkien, Sarah J Maas… Oh, and so many others!'

She rattled off names—his favourites featured among them; he'd never heard of the others, but made a mental note to check them out. It had been too long since he'd read a book, too long since he'd wanted to, but the urge swept through him now.

He clenched his jaw so hard it started to ache. He'd been as guilty as Cleo in cutting joy from his life, but he wasn't giving up reading for anyone. A man was allowed one comfort.

'That wasn't supposed to make you mad.'

He glanced up to find Cleo biting her lip, dismay etching lines into her lovely face. 'I'm not mad at you, I'm mad at myself,' he said.

Before she could ask why, he rushed on. 'This is amazing, Cleo. You're very talented.'

'Thank you. Like I said, it was fun. Though, of course, my ulterior motive is to spur you on to write the last book. I *so* want to read this series!'

He knew she said it to lighten the moment, but he couldn't laugh; he couldn't even smile. Write the last book? Impossible.

*You sure?*

She clapped her hands. 'Your turn.'

He dragged his mind back to the gratitude list. What the hell was the last item on his list? He contemplated using one of her old chestnuts and saying he was grateful he had his health and a place to sleep. But, no matter how much he wanted to, he couldn't do it. She'd given so much of herself. It wouldn't be fair.

'After I say it, there's to be no questions, no discussion...nothing.'

'Okay.'

He dragged in a breath. 'For the first time in nine months, it didn't hurt to talk about writing.' He still couldn't get his head around it. 'I'm grateful for that.'

Her jaw dropped, her eyes widening with a hundred questions, but true to her word she didn't utter a single one. And then she smiled, a beaming light of a smile that felt like the beginning of a fairy tale.

His phone buzzed. Picking it up, he read the message and, rising, he handed her the laptop. 'The car is here early.'

# CHAPTER SEVEN

NERVES JANGLED IN Cleo's stomach. 'It's an hour early.'

Jude's phone buzzed again. He read the message and shrugged. 'Things are moving more quickly than expected.'

*Um...okay.* Trying to look composed, she stowed her laptop into the tote bag, donned the blonde wig and settled a beanie over it.

'What are we going to do with the perishables?' She gestured to the fridge and the pears on the kitchen bench.

'Leave them.'

'Which means you'll come back to—'

'There's not much left and I've a caretaker coming in to look after things.'

*He did?*

'Though we're not leaving the banana bread.'

Reaching across, he seized the banana bread and wrapped it in wax-proof paper and a clean tea towel.

'Here, put this on.'

She caught the mac he tossed to her and shrugged it on. He swung her tote bag over his shoulder, picked up the small case he'd packed for himself and stowed the banana bread under his arm.

'We're in luck. It's started to rain.' He pushed an umbrella into her hands. 'As soon as we reach the top of the stairs, open it and keep as much of your face behind it as you can. I'll go first. Just keep your eyes on my feet and follow.'

'Is there something you're not telling me?'

He swung back.

'Am I about to be greeted with the flashes of a hundred cameras?' If she was, she'd rather know that now.

'There aren't any journalists waiting to pounce on us, but after what happened earlier I'm taking every precaution; that's all this is about.'

*Right.*

'Ready?'

'Yes.'

They exited *Camelot*, and she followed him along a dock and across a small yard to a waiting car—big, black with tinted windows. Not that she got a good look at it. Jude ushered her before him, taking the still open umbrella and shielding her as she slid inside the car's luxurious interior, before following her.

She stared at him as the car pulled away on silent wheels. 'Have you worked as a bouncer or

bodyguard? Because you did that like a professional.' It reminded her of her acting days when
she'd been filming on location.

He sent her a wry smile. 'No.'

'Where are we going?'

His phone buzzed with an incoming text. He
read it and grimaced. 'At the moment we're heading to the airport. The rest I'm still trying to sort
out.'

*The airport? Oh, God.* He was going full Jason
Diamond heroic on her. This had to be costing
him a fortune. Reaching across, she squeezed his
forearm. 'I want you to know that my rainy-day
fund is at your full disposal.' She'd cover whatever costs she could.

Glancing up from his phone, something in his
face softened. 'Cleo...'

The phone rang and he blew out a breath. 'I
have to answer this.'

When they reached the airport she was ushered onto a private jet. Before she could splutter
out a single question, Jude disappeared into the
cockpit. From then, for all intents and purposes,
they travelled separately. When the jet set down
in Nice, two bodyguards ushered her to another
car with tinted windows, drove her down to the
harbour and escorted her onto a super-yacht.

*A super-yacht!*

She was shown into a saloon and the yacht immediately headed out of the harbour. She had no idea if Jude was on board or not.

Half an hour later, he strode into the saloon wearing an exquisitely tailored suit that fitted him to perfection, highlighting his broad shoulders and strong thighs. It was so unexpected, her jaw dropped.

Grimacing, he shrugged out of his jacket and irritably flicked open the top two buttons of the crisp white business shirt, like some kind of movie star. Her mouth dried while her pulse surged in giddy appreciation.

*Don't.*

She dragged her gaze away. She couldn't afford to indulge a single carnal thought where this man was concerned. As previous experience had proved, she was a terrible judge when it came to romantic partners. And he was just too *tempting.* Just… *No.*

He poured himself a Scotch from the polished blond-wood bar at the far end of the room, before sauntering down to sit directly across from her on the semicircular sofa—a bespoke white leather indulgence that fitted the curve of the room.

An acre of space spread between them— literally *and* figuratively. She lifted her hands. 'Who are you?'

Hooded eyes stared back. 'You didn't look me up on the Internet?'

It hadn't occurred to her to do any such thing. 'Is Jude Blackwood another pseudonym?'

Seizing his glass, he moved to sit beside her. Not too close, but close enough that she could see the exhausted lines fanning out from his eyes. Something in her chest clenched.

'Not a pseudonym, but my name isn't well known in England.' He sipped his drink. 'You've heard of Cesar Giroux?'

Everyone had heard of the Giroux family, though Cesar had died four years ago. 'What does he have to do with you?'

He stared into his Scotch. 'Cesar was my grandfather.'

Her eyes bugged. *No way.*

'*You're* the Giroux heir?'

The Giroux family were French industrialists who'd made their fortune several generations ago, and had been adding to it ever since. They were one of the richest families in France, feted wherever they went. Cesar had been nicknamed 'Midas', because everything he'd touched had turned to gold.

Random snippets of news reports came to her: Cesar's state funeral; the shocking death of the older brother, Matthew—Jude's brother; his mother, Cesar's only child, dying of a drug overdose when Jude had been a young boy; one of Cesar's nieces marrying a Scandinavian royal. The family was wealthy, powerful and influential, and their fortune legendary.

Her cheeks burned. 'I offered the *Giroux heir* the use of my rainy-day fund to help finance our escape? *Seriously?*'

'Cleo—'

'And when I crashed onto your boat and inferred you were living frugally and that some extra money might come in handy…' As if he'd been living a hand-to-mouth existence—how he must've laughed.

*Floor, swallow me now.*

Reaching out, he took her hand. 'You treated me like a real person. You judged me on our interactions rather than my family's fortune. You treated me like you would anyone else. I treasured that.'

The expression in his eyes had her heart flipping. She carefully reclaimed her hand and eased back a fraction, things inside her becoming too heated and needy.

'I wasn't trying to deceive you. I was just…enjoying my anonymity. I'm sorry I didn't tell you who I was sooner.'

She waved that away. 'Totally understandable.' She'd have done the same in his place.

'So…you don't want to throw your drink in my face or punch me?'

She tried to glare but failed. 'It should be too soon for that joke.'

He gave one of those crooked half-smiles that never failed to send her insides into a spin. She recalled that moment earlier when his lips had found hers...

She jerked back, horror dawning through her. 'You're *seriously* famous.' He was ten times the news story she was. 'You have to be one of Europe's most eligible bachelors. You—' she gestured at him and then to herself '—and me. If we're photographed together...' It would create a sensation of *monumental* proportions.

'I know.' Tilting his head back, he drained the contents of his glass. 'But you forget I've also the kind of wealth that can shield you from the media. And I'm going to use every tool at my disposal to do exactly that. I assure you, Cleo, no one is going to discover where you are and who you're with. You have my word.'

The yacht was amazing. When Jude took her for the grand tour the following morning, Cleo spent most of it trying to haul her jaw off the floor. Besides the spacious saloon with its opulent white leather sofa and blond-wood bar, there was an oak panelled dining room, a galley kitchen that was thrice the size of *Camelot*'s, and eight bedrooms, all with *en suites*. There was an office-cum-library and a gym.

There were staff quarters on a lower deck. There was a magnificent pool at the stern. There was a hot tub on the main deck, and the upper deck had a sky lounge—all clear glass and marvellous light. There were myriad outdoor seating and dining areas. As soon as the first helicopter flew overhead, though, she avoided all of those, along with the sky lounge. She couldn't get the image of a telescopic lens out of her mind.

She and Jude fell into a kind of rhythm. Because the yacht was operating on a skeleton staff, she continued to cook while he ate with the same relish he'd shown on *Camelot*. They worked out in the gym, and they set up their laptops in the yacht's generous office.

They danced around each other trying to act normal, *very* careful not to touch. Yet every now and again she'd glance up and catch an expression in his eyes—an expression of heat and yearning, sweetened with a strange tenderness. And her reaction was always instant and totally out of proportion—her skin would prickle with a heat that made her fidget, made her antsy. And it wasn't the kind of antsy that a hard session in the gym could ease.

*No men. No romance. No making headlines.*

She kept repeating it silently, like a mantra. She wasn't going to let herself down. She wasn't going to let her family down. And she wasn't going to let Jude down either. *Nothing* could happen between them.

\* \* \*

'You don't have a French accent.'

It was their fourth morning on the yacht and Cleo was pounding the treadmill while Jude's legs furiously pumped the stationary bicycle.

'Didn't you grow up in France?'

He wore shorts and his thigh muscles bunched and flexed. Her mouth went dry. With an effort, she dragged her gaze away. She had no idea how to mitigate the intensity of her *want*. She wanted him, with a fierceness that made no sense. She did her best not to think about it and tried to focus her mind on other things. Yet she'd constantly jerk back into the moment, realising she'd been indulging in flagrantly detailed fantasies of making love with him: slow sensual love-making; fast, furious love-making. Intense love-making…

She couldn't remember ever wanting anyone with this kind of intensity.

In perfectly accented French, Jude now said, 'My French is flawless.'

*'Oui,'* she agreed.

'My parents divorced when I was six and my British father insisted that Matt and I be educated in England. We spent most of our school holidays at the Château Giroux, though.'

She'd seen photographs of the château, located on the outskirts of Paris. It took grandeur to a whole new level.

'I was close to my maternal grandparents before they passed.'

She kept her gaze to the front. 'And you were close to your paternal grandmother too.' The one who'd made him promise to do one good thing a day. 'When did you get to spend time with her?'

She couldn't resist a quick glance in his direction to find her question had surprised a smile from him, which made her breath catch.

No, no, that was the exercise. She slowed her pace to ensure oxygen could still reach her bloodstream.

'When my father dumped me and Matt in boarding school, we barely saw him—or my mother. Gran upped sticks from London and moved to the town where the school was located. She insisted we spend every weekend with her.'

'Oh, what a lovely thing to do! She sounds wonderful.'

He nodded. 'She took two rowdy boys, who were pretty angry at the world at the time, in her stride.'

Of course they'd have been angry. They'd been ripped from all they'd known and abandoned.

'She made us into a family,' he finished simply.

Her eyes filled.

'If you start crying, Cleo, I'm throwing you overboard.'

'I'm not crying!' She picked up her pace again. 'You make me jealous. I've no memories of my grandparents.' She sent him a sidelong glance. 'I'm sorry, Jude. You must miss her enormously.'

'I believe you already gave me your condolences.'

The timer dinged and they both stopped, both breathing hard from the exertion. 'But now I know more about her, which means my condolences are more.'

'More what?'

'Just…more.'

Climbing off the treadmill, she reached for her towel and pressed it to her face and neck. Glancing across, she found Jude's hungry gaze glued to where she'd blotted the towel to her throat. The racing of her pulse nearly brought her to her knees. She deliberately turned away.

'What about your dad?' *Breathe, Cleo, breathe.* 'Do you ever see him?'

'He died when I was sixteen. A lorry blew a tyre on the motorway and slammed into his car.'

She swung back, her heart sinking. 'Oh, Jude, how awful.'

He rolled his shoulders. 'We weren't close.'

'That doesn't make any difference. It's worse in some ways, because now you'll never know what the future could've held.'

He stared, and for a moment she thought he might say more, but then he shook his head and ushered her through the door. 'I need a cold drink before hitting the shower. You?'

She nodded.

'It must be time for you to answer a few questions for a change. What about you? Were you close to your mum?'

Oh, God. Had she been asking too many questions? Of course she had. She needed to stop doing that...

'Cleo?'

Jude's eyes narrowed at the way Cleo had started frown.

She shook herself. 'Yes, really close.'

Hence the reason Cleo had gone off the rails so spectacularly after she'd died, he supposed. He handed her a bottle of water from the bar in the saloon and sprawled on the sofa. 'What was she like?'

'Smart, vibrant, fun. We didn't know what to do after we lost her.'

She paced around the room, her gaze fixed on the view outside. 'She brought out the best in us. She made Dad talkative, when he's not the most communicative of men. Margot has a tendency to be a bit too serious, and she got her to laugh and be a bit silly. She made them relax and have fun.'

She smiled, remembering, but she was still too keyed up, too tense. This woman needed to learn to relax. 'Cleo, sit. You've just spent an hour pounding away in the gym.'

She shook her head. 'I'm not sweating my dirty sweat all over your white sofa.'

'Why not?'

'Respect.'

'It's hard-wearing and easy to clean,' he shot back. 'And I insist.'

After the briefest of hesitations, she perched on the very edge of a seat. But he suspected she'd only done it to humour him. Maybe talking more about her mum would help her unwind. 'How did your mum bring out the best in you?'

She sent him a sidelong glance. 'You might not believe it, but I was a shy teenager. Mum brought me out of my shell. Acting was her idea; she thought me joining a drama group would help me gain confidence.'

Confidence she'd lost when her mother had died. His heart went out to her.

She tapped a finger against her water bottle. 'You know, we've never really functioned properly as a family since.'

She stood again, strode across to the bank of windows and stared out at the view—at the hills of Nice rising up behind the terracotta tiles of the city. The sun glittered off a sea that sparkled silver and blue. 'I can't believe how beautiful it is here.'

'Come up on deck.' It was January, so it was cold, but not like in London or Paris. She'd been cooped up for too long. The fresh air would do her good.

She shook her head.

'Why not?'

'There are other yachts.' She pointed.

They were miles away!

She then pointed skywards. 'And haven't you heard the helicopters passing overhead?'

Was she worried they might be news helicopters?

'Anyway, I'm content inside.' She gave an excited wiggle. 'Do you know how amazing this is?' She turned on the spot, her eyes filled with a mix of awe and delight, and something in his chest softened. Some silly thing he did his best to ignore.

'I feel as if I've been rewarded for my bad behaviour—land myself on the front pages and get whisked away to the French Riviera.'

'Or maybe you were rewarded for sticking up for yourself. Clay deserved everything he got.' Reaching out, he gently squeezed her shoulders, her warmth flooding every pore. 'You deserve every drop of good fortune that comes your way, Cleo.'

She stared at him as if his words had momentarily immobilised her. Her gaze lowered to his mouth. Full lips parted, as if parched.

Hunger roared in his ears. To taste those lips one more time…

Cleo tugged herself free, leaving his hands empty. She backed up a step, and then another one, her eyes not meeting his. She pointed behind her. 'I…uh…shower.' Turning, she fled.

He clenched his hands at his sides and counted to twenty until he was certain she'd reached her cabin before heading to his own. His punishing cold shower should've left him blue, but barely took the edge off the heat banked just below the surface of his skin. He needed to tread carefully— very carefully. He'd sworn to himself that he wouldn't get involved with Cleo. It was just too… dangerous. There was a warmth beneath his desire that instinct told him would lead to trouble of the heartache variety. He wasn't opening himself up to that, no matter how much he wanted her, or how much he liked her.

He'd been burned before, and he wasn't interested in repeating the experience. Nor was he interested in opening himself up to the agonies Elodie now suffered.

While Cleo was doing her best to get her act together, what would happen the next time life dealt her a blow? Would she act with maturity, or not? What if he unintentionally provided that life blow? A bad taste coated his tongue. Their attraction had the potential to be monumentally destructive, materially and emotionally. His body might burn for her, but he'd burn in hell if he gave into the temptation.

\* \* \*

'Okay.' Cleo put down her book—the third in the Jason Diamond series—and clapped her hands. 'Gratitude time.'

He held up his puzzle book. 'I finished the cryptic crossword.'

He'd had his staff grab a host of puzzle books from the airport. Just as they had on *Camelot*, he and Cleo continued to do identical puzzles and compared notes at the end of the day.

'No way! I need a clue for three down. It completely bamboozled me.'

She was a novice when it came to puzzles, but was smart and quick. Given enough time, he suspected she'd overtake him. Not that they'd be here long enough for that.

Stretching, he shifted on his seat. 'Go on, then, hit me with your gratitude list.' He wouldn't say he looked forward to doing this gratitude thing, but he'd started to find it easier. And the way her eyes lit up when she listed her items was a definite consolation.

'My beef stew was perfection.'

His mouth watered at the memory. 'It was.'

'I don't always get it right, but I did tonight, which was satisfying.'

He searched his mind for something to add to his list. 'I fixed an engine problem. It was a bit tricky, but it worked.'

She stared. He half-scowled. 'What? If you can

have beef stew, then there's nothing wrong with me putting engine repairs on my list.'

'Absolutely *nothing* wrong with it. I thought you'd have an engineer for that.'

He did, but engines were another kind of puzzle, and he liked to tinker.

'It's just, you're so…*capable.*'

Their gazes locked and the air between shimmered. It took all his strength to wrench his away and lift his glass of whisky to his lips.

'I added a book page to the Jay Ballimore website.'

He glanced back.

'It was fun. Want me to send it to you?'

He stalked across to the bar and poured himself another finger of whisky. 'Sure, why not?'

'Say please.'

Her teasing made it hard not to grin. 'Cleo, could you please send me the new website page that you made today? I'm curious to see it.'

She wriggled in her seat. 'That acknowledgement almost makes my list, but I'm afraid it's trumped by Margot.'

He started to walk back to his seat but froze at her words. With an effort of will, he made his legs move again. 'That sounds…' *Promising? Ominous?* He sat. He had no idea.

'I've been emailing her every day with my gratitude list. Today she emailed back with hers. Nothing else, no other message, but it's a start.'

He swore.

She blinked. 'Did you just say *a very rude word*?'

He glared. 'Must you always over-share?'

She crossed her arms, her shoulders inching up towards her ears. 'It feels safe to share here. I...'

'It's not a criticism.' Her confidences made him feel privileged. He scowled: and beholden.

'I'm in awe, that's all,' he grouched. 'You seem to find it easy.'

She sent him the smallest of smiles. 'What happens on a super-yacht remains on a super-yacht. Same goes for narrow boats.'

Dragging in a breath, he nodded. 'I'm pleased you're making progress with Margot.' That was huge news.

'Thank you.'

She stared at him expectantly. His scowl deepened. 'Okay, there's to be no response to what I'm about to say, got it?'

'Okay.'

'I started the first chapter in book three of my fantasy series.'

Her eyes widened. Her hands slapped to her thighs. She leaned towards him...

He pointed. 'Not a single word.'

Her mouth snapped shut. Without uttering a word, she happy-danced, then she picked up her Jason Diamond book and opened it to the bookmarked page.

He couldn't have said why, but it made him smile. 'That's great news about Margot, Cleo.'

She didn't look up. 'Thank you.'

'The website page...?'

'Already sent.'

Margot was talking to Cleo again. He had to double every effort and ensure nobody discovered where she was. He wouldn't let anyone ruin this for her.

As for the writing... What the hell did he think he was doing? When he took his place as head of the Giroux family, there'd be no time for writing. There'd be only duty and responsibility. Duty and responsibility he had no intention of shirking ever again.

# CHAPTER EIGHT

'THE POOL IS HEATED, Cleo. You can go for a swim if you want.'

Cleo turned away from the window with its view of the pool. It wasn't a plunge pool, but a proper pool—one any resort would be proud of. She suspected she'd been staring at it a little too wistfully. 'It's just hard to not keep admiring the view. I mean, the Côte d'Azur! I have to keep pinching myself.'

No matter how much she might want to, she couldn't go for a swim, even though there was a wardrobe of clothes in her cabin, including swimsuits. The pool was on the open deck, and helicopters continued to pass overhead with monotonous regularity.

She was Cleo Milne. Jude was the Giroux heir. And together they'd be tabloid gold. Margot deserved better from her. *Jude* deserved better from her.

He stood. 'Come on.'

'I'm not swimming, Jude.' It was too risky.

'I'm not talking about the pool.'

*Another session in the gym? Excellent idea!* Powering down her computer, she followed him. But he didn't lead her to the gym; instead, he led her to… *The hot tub? No way!*

Turning on the jets, he took her hand and plunged it into the water. 'Feel how warm that is.'

She nearly swooned. It was heaven.

Releasing her, he pointed to the awning above. 'This area is covered.' He pressed a button on the wall and shade screens lowered. 'A telescopic lens isn't getting through that lot.'

Still, she hesitated. It was hard enough being in the same room as Jude, working at different ends of the huge table in the yacht's office or sitting on opposite sides of the curved white sofa in the saloon, let alone jumping into a hot tub with him.

'You said you wanted more joy in your life. And yet here you are, still turning your back on it.'

'No, I'm not!'

'And I can't help wondering why.'

She rubbed both hands over her face. 'Because I don't want to keep making the same mistakes.'

He blinked.

'Surely you understand that? I want to find joy responsibly. I don't want to keep looking for it in the wrong places.' Especially not in the lead up to Margot's wedding. She couldn't afford to be reckless or rash.

He folded his arms. 'It's just a hot tub, Cleo.'

Which of course made her feel like a fool.

'And there's no chance of the paparazzi snapping a picture of you here.'

Even to her paranoid eyes, all looked safe.

'And I dare you.'

'You...*what*?'

He raised an eyebrow.

The hot tub was huge. Hitching up her chin, she pointed to it. 'I'll meet you here in ten.'

He was already in the tub when she returned, a cocktail glass in one hand, the picture of relaxed, and *potent*, masculinity. An identical glass rested nearby for her. 'But I don't...'

'Mocktail,' he said.

He'd made her a mocktail? That was kind of... sweet. Self-consciousness had her momentarily clutching her towelling robe to her chest, which was crazy. She'd worn swimsuits on her TV show. Thousands of people had seen her wearing a bikini. But she'd bet Jude hadn't been one of them.

*Stop it. Get in the hot tub.* Gritting her teeth, she dropped the robe onto a nearby chair and climbed in. Jude studiously glanced away, as if doing his best not to notice. She did her best to not notice him in turn.

Seizing her mocktail, she sipped it, tasting pineapple juice, coconut milk and a hint of lime.

'Delicious.' Setting it to the side and sliding

up to her neck in the water, she closed her eyes and let the heat and bubble jets work their magic.

She didn't open her eyes. 'Okay, I'll admit it—this was an inspired idea.'

'I think we've earned it.'

She opened an eye and peeked at him. The hot tub was built on generous lines, but even from this opposite corner—as far away from him as she could get—the breadth of his shoulders and the golden perfection of his skin beckoned.

His jaw clenched, as if he'd sensed her gaze. Heat of a different kind gathered in all the places she didn't want it to. Gritting her teeth, she forced her eye shut. She wouldn't do anything stupid. She wouldn't do anything reckless or self-defeating. She'd caused enough havoc in Margot's life. Her sister deserved to have the wedding of her dreams. Cleo would hate herself forever if she cast the smallest shadow on the day.

A helicopter passed overhead and she forced herself to imagine worst-case scenarios—such as what would happen if she and Jude were snapped in a hot tub and the photograph plastered across the front pages of the newspapers. A slavering horde of paparazzi would then trail in her wake, catcalling and disrupting everything with their pointing cameras and impertinent questions. She imagined the hurt and betrayal stretching through Margot's eyes, the way her father's mouth would tighten as if he'd been stupid to expect better from her, and died a little inside. Was a brief fling worth that price? *Hard no.*

Anyway, what was it Jude had called love—an exercise in deception, disillusion and despair? She shuddered. No way was she getting involved with someone with a worldview that bleak.

Which begged its own question. She stared up at the awning. 'Can I ask you something?'

'Hasn't stopped you in the past.'

Her stomach clenched. Had she been bothering him?

'Ask your question, Cleo.'

'It might be considered invasive.'

'I can't wait.'

His assumed nonchalance made her smile. Something had lightened inside him during the last few days and she was glad of it.

'How has your Jasper Ballimore identity remained a secret? How has one of your girlfriends not spilled the beans?'

When he remained silent, she lifted her head to glance at him. 'I told you it was invasive. It's just, girlfriends always have a way of finding things out.'

Turning his head, he raised a wry eyebrow. She forced herself to settle back again. 'Though, unlike me, you probably haven't had a series of disastrous relationships.'

'The problem, Cleo, is when your family is

as wealthy as mine you never know if someone wants you for yourself.'

'Or whether you're a status symbol and a meal ticket.'

'Exactly.'

'Are you saying you've run shy of romantic relationships all your life?'

'It's my MO now.'

Which meant it hadn't been his MO once.

'I've no interest in marrying and being made a fool of.'

Overhead, another helicopter passed by. She couldn't see it, but glared in its direction. 'Was Matt disillusioned in love too?'

'Matt and Elodie were very much in love. But Elodie has been in hell since Matt died. It seems to me that love extracts a price, and it's not one I want to pay.'

It took every effort to not look at him. Someone had hurt him, and had hurt him badly.

'I did contemplate marriage once.'

She swallowed her surprise.

'However, the woman I considered proposing to…'

Had she cheated on him, betrayed him? Her heart clenched. Jude deserved better, and if she got her hands on the woman…

'She discovered my Jasper Ballimore secret and proceeded to name a price to keep it. I got my lawyers on it immediately.'

'The witch!'

'It was a small price to pay to get her out of my life. I'm grateful I didn't make the mistake of marrying her.'

She glanced across. 'I hope she rots in hell.'

He met her gaze and shrugged. 'It was a long time ago.'

The glance grew heated. She dragged hers away and resumed resting back and gazing upwards. That kind of betrayal would have left a mark. No wonder he'd become so cynical. 'I'm sorry you were treated so badly.' She swallowed. 'And thank you for not throwing me immediately off *Camelot* when I told you I'd discovered the secret too.'

'You're nothing like Nicole, Cleo. *You* have a good heart.'

She refused to let his words warm her. Reaching for her glass, she raised it in his direction. 'To a train wreck with a good heart.'

He raised his glass too. 'To good hearts.'

She sipped then set her drink aside. 'What I don't understand is why it's so important for Jasper Ballimore to remain a secret.'

He was quiet for a moment. 'I don't need the money from book sales, which has freed me from the pressures of publicity. I've been fortunate to enjoy the best about being an author without the downsides.'

Some people would have seen the fame as the best part.

'Also, Jasper Ballimore isn't on brand for the Giroux name.'

Not 'on brand'? Did he mean not serious enough? She straightened. 'Says who?' Had this come from his family? 'Your family should be proud of you.'

'They are—those who know about it.'

'So...this is a decision you took on your own?'

'Look.' He sat up. 'With great wealth and privilege comes great responsibility.' He recited it like a lecture. 'I need to carry on my grandfather's legacy. There's no room now for frivolous things like writing. Giroux Holdings is a family corporation. The head of the family needs to work hard to maintain that for the sake of future generations.'

'What? While everyone else suns themselves on a super-yacht?'

He stared, then grinned, as if her outrage tickled him. Her heart did a silly pitter-patter thing. 'Everyone pulls their weight, Cleo. There are no shirkers.'

She mulled that over. 'Being head of the family sounds like a big responsibility.'

'And one I left entirely on Matt's shoulders.' His mouth turned grim. 'The problem is, I inherited my grandfather's Midas touch. When it comes to business, I have his knack for making money.'

But it didn't feed his soul the way writing did. He didn't have to say the words out loud. She could see it for herself.

'Matt, though, encouraged me to pursue what made me happy.' His jaw clenched. 'But in doing that I left him alone to deal with everything. I could've helped him. I *should've* helped him.'

*Oh, Jude.* He held himself responsible for so much.

'That's all nonsense, you know.' She kept her tone conversational, but his glare turned glacial.

'You're not responsible for what happened to Matt. And being head of Giroux Holdings doesn't mean you can't write. You're the boss now, you can arrange things however you want. You don't have to play the martyr.'

His jaw dropped.

'If Matt had asked for your help, would you have denied him?'

'Of course not. I—'

'Did Matt hate being the head of the family?'

'That's beside the point.'

*It so wasn't.* 'Don't make the same mistakes your brother did, Jude. Change things so your nephew never feels as hemmed in and restricted as you now do.'

His lips twisted. 'Ah, but that's not the traditional way things are done. We're a family who values its traditions.'

'Just because something is traditional doesn't mean it's good. Innovation has its place.' She flicked water at him. 'You want your nephew to be happy, don't you?'

'What the hell kind of question is that?'

She spread her hands. 'So change things to suit you all. You could establish a family committee to share the load. I bet you have uncles and cousins who have the necessary skills and would love more responsibility.'

She could see him mulling that over for two-tenths of a second. 'That would bring its own problems.'

'There will always be problems. No system is perfect.'

He glared. 'What else do you see in this utopia of yours?'

But the heat had left his voice and she bit back a smile. 'You might have to remain the titular head, but you can delegate, delegate, delegate.'

He rolled his eyes.

'You'd work part-time for Giroux Holdings and spend the other half writing. That way, you wouldn't be neglecting your responsibilities *or* what feeds your soul.' He'd be abdicating neither duty nor joy. 'In keeping the latter, you'll be better at the former.'

'That doesn't necessarily follow, you know?'

'I think it does. Anyway… *I dare you.*'

He rolled his eyes. 'Some people will hate the idea.'

'But I bet your nephew's generation will thank you.'

They were both sitting rather than reclining. It gave her the most spectacular view of his shoulders and chest—his *naked* shoulders and chest. Her bikini-clad breasts were visible above the water line too, and she noted the way he carefully averted his gaze. Her skin drew tight and fire raced through her veins. She forced herself back into a reclining position, sinking her entire body below the waterline. *Breathe*. 'What would Matt have thought of the idea?'

He didn't answer, not that she expected him to.

Overhead yet another helicopter passed. She glared. It was better than focussing on thoughts of hurling herself at Jude. She pointed skyward. 'What do you think they're hoping to find?'

Without warning, Jude rose and stepped out of the hot tub in a single lithe movement. Water sluiced down his body, his trunks plastered to the most glorious pair of glutes she'd ever seen. Her mouth went dry. She'd never wanted with the kind of want she now did. The man was *beautiful*.

'Out of the hot tub, Cleo.'

Her heart lurched into her throat. Had he seen…?

'We're leaving.'

Her heart settled back to beat erratically in her chest. 'Leaving?'

He gestured at the helicopter. 'It was a mistake coming here. I thought you'd be able to relax.'

'I am! Jude, you don't need to—'

'We're leaving for the Château Giroux. It's where I should've taken you in the first place.'

# CHAPTER NINE

THEY DROVE THROUGH the iron gates of Château
Giroux at seven o'clock that evening. Clean lines
graced the palatial four-storey façade and four elegant towers rose at each corner. Cleo stared at
the fairy-tale elegance and had no words.

Outside it was all white stone walls and black
slate roof. Inside it was white marble and soar-
ing ceilings, the walls lined with works of art in-
termingled with what she assumed were family
portraits. There was elegant furniture, exquisite
Aubusson rugs and antiques stretched for as far
as the eye could see.

'It's beautiful.' She breathed, staring around,
trying to take it all in.

The housekeeper sent her a smile as she led
them up the grand staircase to a room at the top
of the stairs, an enormous drawing room. A fire
crackled in the fireplace and the furniture, while
grand, had clearly been chosen for comfort. A
little boy, maybe three or four years old, leapt to
his feet, shouting, 'Uncle Jude!'

Racing across the room, he launched himself at the man beside her. Jude caught him easily and swung him into the air. The childish giggles made her smile.

After a hug and more tossing, Jude set the boy on his feet and turned him to Cleo. 'Oliver, this is my friend Cleo.'

Cleo held out her hand. 'I'm very pleased to meet you, Oliver.'

Oliver shook it. 'Are you going to marry Uncle Jude?'

She choked back a laugh, but for the life of her couldn't meet Jude's eyes. She fought to keep her tone light. 'Well, Oliver, as much as I like your uncle, I expect not. We're just very good friends.'

'Would you like to see my truck?'

'Yes, please, very much.'

Before he could haul Cleo across the other side of the room, though, a woman rose from one of the sofas arranged near the fire. 'Oliver, come here.' Her voice was sharp. 'Do not bother the lady.'

'It's no bother,' Cleo assured her. 'I like trucks almost as much as I like boats.'

The little boy grinned at her. The woman did not.

The touch of Jude's hand at the small of her back urged her forward and had warmth curling in her abdomen and circling lower in ever more concentrated circles. It took all her concentration to make her legs work. The burning, the need and want remained long after he'd removed his hand.

'Cleo, this is my sister-in-law, Elodie.'

'Pleased to meet you.'

'Delighted,' said the other woman, though her frosty gaze declared otherwise.

Cleo glanced at Jude. His clenched jaw and flared nostrils told their own story. A woman, presumably a nanny, entered to take Oliver to bed. The little boy kissed his mother, hugged his uncle and promised to show Cleo his truck in the morning.

'You're looking well, Elodie.'

'What are you doing here, Jude? You know I don't want you here. You're not welcome.'

Not welcome? But this was his home.

Cleo stepped forward. 'I needed a bolthole. Jude has very kindly played the hero and brought me here to hide from the paparazzi.'

At Elodie's questioning eyebrow, Cleo explained how Jude had helped her to hide from the paparazzi when they'd been chasing her.

'And how long are you planning to stay?'

Elodie directed the question at Jude, but Cleo pretended it had been meant for her. Lifting her arms, she turned on the spot. 'Now that I've seen the Château Giroux, I'm thinking forever.'

The light-hearted words were meant to dispel the tension, but they fell disappointingly flat. Elodie turned burning dark eyes in Cleo's direction.

'As for Jude playing hero? I find that unlikely.'
And then she was gone.

Cleo's stomach dropped to her feet as pieces
of the puzzle fell into place. It wasn't just Jude
who blamed himself for Matt's death—Elodie
did too. And the expression on Jude's face made
her want to weep.

*Don't hug him. Don't hug him. Don't hug him.*

But not hugging him with the hardest thing
she'd ever done. Swallowing, she kept her chin
high. 'Aren't families grand? This reminds me
of Christmas four years ago. It was a real barrel
of laughs.'

A huff of a laugh left him. 'You're…'

'Let's settle on "incorrigible". It's more endear-
ing than "irresponsible" or "irreverent"—which
happen to be two of my father's favourite words
when referring to me. Oliver is a sweetheart,' she
added. 'He adores you.'

'It's mutual. Elodie, though…not so much.'

'Who'd have guessed your family would be so
much like mine?'

'Let's not compare war wounds, Cleo.'

She was a guest in his house. She'd do whatever
she could to make their time here as comfortable
for him as possible.

'Let's eat.'

As if he'd magicked them from the woodwork,
staff entered and set a table at the far end of the
room with steaming bowls of French onion soup

and slices of French bread topped with bubbling cheese.

Her stomach rumbled its approval, and one of those beguiling chuckles rumbled from Jude's throat to trace a tempting finger down her spine. She did her very best to ignore it. Instead, she chattered about mundane things until some of the darkness had receded from his eyes.

As had become their habit, they retired early. She'd never slept in such a luxurious room. She should've slept like a log, and yet she tossed and turned, yearning for the sound of lapping water and the slight rocking of a boat.

Jude's and her bedrooms shared a sitting room. On *Camelot* they'd been physically closer—they'd been able to hear each other moving about and talking in their sleep—and yet the knowledge that he was only two doors away…shouldn't be more tempting, more intimate. But that was exactly what it felt like.

*Don't think about it.* Instead, she replayed that moment when Jude had leapt out of the hot tub with the decision to bring her here to the Château Giroux. Because he wanted her to relax, to let down her guard, to feel completely safe.

She could see now why he'd stayed away. And yet he'd come here anyway…*for her.* It was one of the kindest, most stupidly unselfish things anyone had ever done for her, an act of open-handed generosity that created a warm glow at her very centre.

He was the most amazing man.

And he was only two doors away.

*Don't think about it.*

After another hour of tossing and turning, she gave up. Grabbing a throw and her book, she padded out to the living room. She pulled up short when she found Jude staring moodily into the embers that were dying down in the small grate.

He glanced across. 'Can't sleep?'

Dropping her book onto the coffee table, she arranged herself at the other end of the sofa, drawing her feet up, careful not to touch him. 'The bed is exceptionally comfortable, and I should be dead to the world, but...'

'You never sleep well the first night in a new place.'

She stared. He remembered...

He shrugged. 'It's an interesting character trait.'

She tried not to read anything into it. 'So what's your excuse?'

He turned back to the fire. 'Too many ghosts.'

'Matt,' she murmured softly.

'He and Elodie made their home here after they married.'

'And you?'

'My grandmother moved back to London when Matt and I finished school. I split my time between here and my flat in London.'

He hadn't wanted to abandon his grandmother. Her stomach softened.

'I have an apartment overlooking the Thames.'

Of course he did. They both stared into the fire. 'And yet you banished yourself to *Camelot* for the last seven months.'

'Not banished—I wanted peace and quiet. Wanted room to breathe.'

She understood that he'd needed to adjust to the new reality of life without his brother, but in his grief and misplaced guilt it seemed he'd shut himself away from everyone.

She turned to face him more fully. Inside her were things with jagged edges. 'When was the last time you were at the Château Giroux?'

'The day we buried Matt.'

She wanted to weep. 'Have you stayed away because of Elodie?'

He nodded. 'It's hard for her to see me.'

And then she was on her knees and so close the heat from his body beat at her. 'It's not fair of her to blame you for your brother's death, Jude. Or to punish you like this.'

'She has every right!' His eyes flashed. 'I should've realised Matt had been drinking. I should've taken the car keys from him. I should've insisted we take a cab home. I—'

'None of it was your fault!'

Her words rang around the room. Surely his

grandmother had told him this, his cousins and friends? But maybe he hadn't been ready to listen.

'Jude, it was an *accident.*' He opened his mouth but she rode on over the top of him. 'It wasn't your fault Matt had been drinking. Of course you believed him when he told you he hadn't been. He probably thought he was fine to drive.'

He stared at her.

'And it wasn't either your or Matt's fault a deer raced across the road when it did. An *accident,*' she repeated. *'Nobody's* fault.'

His lips twisted. It took all of her strength not to reach out and touch him.

'And, as for feeling guilty about not having helped out more with the family business… Matt had a tongue in his head. If he'd needed help, he could've asked.'

'That doesn't change the fact—'

'Maybe not, but beating yourself up about it changes nothing. Nor is it fair of Elodie to blame you for it. You miss Matt too.'

'Yes, but…'

She pressed a finger to his lips. 'You can help now, though. There are some things you can do. For one, you owe it to Matt to have a relationship with Oliver.'

Eyes the colour of a turbulent sea throbbed into hers.

'And you can help Elodie move past this, Jude. Her hurt and bitterness are understandable, but it's hurting her. She clings to it because she's scared, because it's easier to be angry than to be heartbroken, but it'll eat her alive.'

He gripped her hand like a lifeline. 'How do you know this?'

Sitting back on her heels, she pulled in a breath. 'They didn't call me Wild Child for nothing. All of those late-night parties, all of the drinking and acting out—that was me trying to run away from my grief for my mother. Therapy helped me see that, helped me realise how self-destructive I was being. When I stopped doing those things and faced my emotions…'

He leaned towards her. Their faces were so close she could feel his breath on her lips and her heart stuttered in her chest.

'What?'

She had to swallow before she could speak. 'It let the good stuff back in. I began to remember the good memories. I started to feel hopeful.' She let out a shaky breath. 'I found a purpose, something to work towards, and I found a way to live with the grief.'

'You think I can help Elodie overcome her anger, and her resentment of me?' He shook his head. 'That's impossible.'

'It's not impossible, not for you. I know you don't see it, but you're amazing. Seems to me you can achieve just about anything you put your mind to.'

His jaw sagged. He hauled it back into place, his gaze throbbing into hers. Oh, so slowly, his gaze lowered to her lips. Hunger blazed in his eyes and things inside her throbbed to life.

She broke all the rules. Leaning forward, she kissed him.

The warm magic of Cleo's lips had heat filling Jude's every pore. He wondered now if this had been inevitable.

Sitting in the hot tub with her had been torture. Trying to look unmoved had taken all his strength. He'd been aware of her tension. Aware of the heat in her gaze when it had rested on him; her curiosity; her interest; her restraint.

And the way she'd tensed every time a helicopter had passed overhead... He'd focused on *that* rather than everything else. It had been the one thing he *could* act upon.

He'd hoped coming here would diminish what was happening between them. But he wondered now if they'd been building to this from the first moment she'd clattered onto his narrowboat.

He sank into the kiss like a starving man. Threading his fingers through her hair, he kissed her with an intensity he had no hope of tempering, and with a thoroughness he hoped told her what an extraordinary woman he thought her. Cleo gave so much of herself with no expectation of anything in return. With her silly, light-hearted teasing, her gratitude lists and her frank confessions, she'd felled all of his barriers. *And* she'd given him hope.

Her fingers tangled in his hair, pulling him closer, and fire blazed in his veins. Pulling her onto his lap, he pressed a series of kisses along her jaw and down her neck, her skin satin-soft, and she hummed her approval, the sound arcing straight to his groin.

Slow hands traced a path along his shoulders and down his chest, sparking heat and intensifying need. Cupping her breast in his hand, relishing its weight, he stroked his thumb across it and her nipple beaded to hardness with flattering speed. It had him hungry to draw it into his mouth, to touch her with his tongue. To taste her…to have her naked beneath him and arching into his touch, crying out his name…

He froze.

*What was he doing?*

'Oh, no, you don't.'

Cleo's ragged whisper scraped across his raw nerve endings. She straddled his lap and he had to force back a groan at the way her body slid against his with an intimacy that left him dry mouthed. His fingers dug into the soft flesh of her hips, though whether it was to anchor her there or to put her away from him when he found the strength to do so he had no idea.

Seizing his face in her hands, pale green eyes

stared into his. 'Why are you hesitating? I know you want me, Jude. As much as I want you.'

He couldn't deny it, not with the evidence of his desire throbbing against her. He clenched his teeth and forced himself to breathe through the red heat. 'You came to me for help.'

'And you don't want to take advantage of me?' A dimple appeared in her right cheek.

'You said sleeping with anyone at the moment would be self-destructive. I don't want to do something that will have you hating yourself in the morning.'

Her smile faded. 'I don't leap into bed with men I barely know any more, Jude. I no longer use sex—or alcohol—as a way to hide from my problems. And you're not just *anyone.*'

His heart gave a kick that knocked the breath from his body.

'I know we only met a bit over a week ago, but we've spent every waking hour of that time together.'

True enough. He'd shared things with her he'd never shared with anyone.

'I know you better than some guys I've dated for months.'

*Like that jerk Clayton Carruthers?*

'What's more, I like you. And I think you like me.'

'Of course I like you!' Meeting this woman had changed his life. He was writing again. Whatever

decision he made in regard to it, it was still a consolation of sorts. His heart kicked again—hard.
She made him think it might be possible to fix
things between Elodie and him.

'This thing—' she gestured between them
'—isn't about me forgetting my troubles for a
night or two.'

'What is it, then, Cleo?'

She braced her hands on his shoulders, smooth-
ing the material of his soft cotton T-shirt over his
arms. 'I like you and I want you. Neither one of
us is in a relationship. We're free to indulge in a
fling. I know you're not interested in a long-term
relationship, so don't think I'll be mistaking this
for anything more than what it is.'

He wasn't interested in anything long-term. He
felt too broken at the moment; his life was going
through too much change. Besides, parading any
kind of coupledom happiness in front of a still
grieving Elodie... It was out of the question. But
a short-term fling...?

'This will be fun and pleasure and tenderness...' A smile trembled on her lips. 'And a
happy memory.'

*He* would be a happy memory for this extraordinary woman! A fault line opened in his chest,
letting in light and warmth.

She patted his chest with soft hands. 'Now, you
may not feel the same, of course.'

She made as if to move off his lap, but his fingers tightened about her hips. 'I think you're the most amazing woman I've ever met. I burn for you, Cleo.'

She stared at him, her lips parting as if his words had taken her off-guard. Tilting up her chin, he slanted his mouth over hers in a scorching kiss that had her fingers digging into his biceps, before wrapping around his neck. She kissed him back with a fiery enthusiasm that had him breathing hard.

Lifting her in his arms, he strode into his bedroom, kicking the door shut with his heel. Tonight he would be the one to give *to her*. He'd give her body all the pleasure that was in his power to provide. He'd make sure it was a night she'd remember when she was eighty—a memory that would make her smile whenever she thought of it. A good memory she could pull out and hold close whenever she needed to.

He followed her down onto the bed and kissed her deeply, slowly… Restless hands moved across his body, but he tried to ignore them.

'Jude…' She panted. 'I need you.'

'And you're going to have me, sweetheart—in all the ways you want me. But first…'

He flicked open a button on the satin pyjamas the staff had found for her and then another… slowly…until he had the shirt spread out and her beautiful breasts exposed to the air and his gaze. Need roared in his ears but he tamped it down.

A sigh left her as his fingers danced across her skin. 'But first I'm going to savour every delectable inch of you.'

A cry left her lips as his mouth closed over one nipple. He sucked, lathed and traced the shape of her with his mouth and tongue. She arched into his touch, the inarticulate noises in her throat making him hard and hot, yet he refused to rush. Her pyjama top fluttered to the floor as he kissed his way down her body.

He ran his fingers through the damp curls at the juncture of her thighs, teasing and tempting, deliberately avoiding where she most wanted to be touched as he divested her of her pyjama bottoms before kissing his way back up her body—ankles, knees, thighs… When he traced his tongue along the seam of her and circled the most sensitive part of her in slow, lazy strokes, her shocked cry, the way her body lifted, almost undid him.

But the sweet scent of her…the taste of her… the feel of her against his mouth and tongue and arms…

'Jude, I need…'

He slid a finger inside her, her silken flesh tightening around it. 'I have you, sweetheart.' He lapped at her with his tongue, slowly, rhythmically, hypnotically, until, with a cry and his name on her lips, she came.

Once the fluttering of her body had subsided, he eased away, rolled on a condom and lowered himself over her, bearing his weight on his fore-arms. He brushed the hair from her face. Heavy-lidded eyes opened and a sultry smile spread across delectable lips. 'I think I just died and went to heaven.'

He grinned down at her. This woman made him feel like Superman. 'I aim to please.'

Her fingers danced down his body, her fingers wrapping around him. 'You certainly do that.'

That wicked hand moved up and down with a gentle strength and purpose that had air hissing between his teeth. Seizing first her right hand and then the left, he trapped them beside her head.

She pouted up at him. 'Why can't I play too?'

His erection nudged her entrance, she lifted her hips to greet him and they slid together in a single smooth motion.

'Oh!'

Her whimper made him tense. 'Did I hurt you? I—'

'No.' Her head moved restlessly against the pil-low. Tugging her hands free from his, she ran them down his body to dig surprisingly strong fingers into his buttocks and haul him even closer, her legs wrapping around his waist.

'It's just…' Her breathing grew ragged, sawing in and out of her lungs. 'I've never wanted some-one so soon again…after…'

He couldn't not move then. The sensations built between them hard and fast. Her warmth and energy, her very essence, surrounded him like a blessing. She gave a final cry, her muscles clenching around him and then his body followed with a will of its own. His hoarse cry filled the room as a golden heat flooded him and stars burst behind his eyelids. Wave after wave of sensation spiralled through him—deep, intense pleasure—and finally peace.

Jude lay in bed and stared at the ceiling, Cleo a warm bundle curled against his side, and watched the early-morning light filter into the room, appreciating the soft-focus gentleness of it after a night of love-making that had left him feeling remade.

It wasn't just the love-making, though—it was the words Cleo had spoken to him. Words that had hope stirring in his heart.

He might feel guilty that he was alive when his brother was dead, but Cleo was right—the event that had claimed his brother's life had been an accident. He couldn't change it, no matter how much he wanted to. But he remembered the look in Elodie's eyes whenever they'd rested on him…

He felt the searing ache of missing his brother that refused to subside…and his regret that he hadn't helped more with the running of Giroux Holdings, that he hadn't taken some of the responsibility from Matt's shoulders. His lips twisted. Being a scapegoat had given him a role to play.

But that didn't help anyone. It was no healthier than all the younger Cleo's drunken partying.

*Matt would want you to have a relationship with Oliver.* He knew the truth of that on a bone-deep level. He needed to be an admirable role model for his nephew; emotional cowardice wasn't admirable on any level. He also knew Matt would want him to give Elodie all and any support he could.

Cleo had made him see it was time to stop hiding. It was time to fight—to fight for his family in the same way that Cleo fought for hers.

Cleo stirred and a smile curved her lips as she blinked sleep from her eyes. A warm arm slid across his chest and she made a sound of approval. He immediately grew hard.

'Did I mention you have a great body?' she murmured.

'You might've mentioned it once or twice.'

He grinned. She grinned.

'I vote that this thing goes for longer than one night.'

He rolled her over and kissed her. 'I second that vote.'

# CHAPTER TEN

JUDE TAPPED ON the open door of Elodie's private sitting room. Elodie's faced hardened when she turned. 'I don't want to see you. I don't want to speak to you.'

A hard knot formed in his stomach. He had to fight the instinct to turn and leave. Recalling the expression in Cleo's eyes last night, he pushed his shoulders back and nodded. 'I know.'

She blinked.

'The thing is, Elodie, your anger at me and your wish to avoid me don't seem to be helping. You're just as unhappy now as you were nine months ago.'

'Unhappy?' she spat. 'How can I be anything other than *unhappy* when my husband is dead?'

'You're no more *at peace*, then.'

Her eyes flashed. Jude rubbed a hand over his face. 'Running away hasn't worked out so well for me either.'

Striding across, she stabbed a finger at him. 'You don't deserve peace.'

Everything inside him burned. It took all his reserves of strength to remain where he stood rather than removing himself from her presence. When he spoke, his voice emerged low, the strain stretching it thin. 'I know you think blaming me is a way to remain strong, but I'm starting to think the opposite is true. Blaming me is stopping you from moving on. You're using all of your resources to remain angry at me, instead of using them to come to terms with your grief.'

She stared back stonily.

'What I've started to realise is that the truth is preferable to continuing in a lie, even when it isn't palatable.'

He ached to reach out and take her hands or hug her, but she held herself so aloof, he dared not. He could not force her to hear his words, *really* hear them, no matter how much he wanted her to. But he had at least to try.

'I'd do whatever I could to make your life easier, Elodie, but continuing in this lie isn't helping any of us. The fact is, I'm *not* responsible for Matt's death. I didn't know he'd been drinking.'

'The alcohol *had* to have affected him. You should've seen that!'

'I wish it had been evident, but it wasn't. The fact I didn't notice, that I didn't pay more attention, is something I will regret till my dying day.' He swallowed hard. 'But it doesn't change the fact that the accident wasn't my fault.'

She took a step back, her eyes widening.

'I've played it over in my mind so many times. Everything happened so fast—*so fast*. Matt's reaction was pure instinct. I don't know if he'd have done any differently if he hadn't had anything to drink. I don't know if I'd have done anything differently if I'd been behind the wheel.'

He dug his fingers into the hard knot of muscle at his nape. 'I wish he'd told me how much pressure he'd been under at work. I wish he'd asked for my help. I wish even more that he hadn't had to ask. I wish I'd seen it and leaped in to do what I could.' *That* would be the biggest regret of his life.

'What I do know, though, is that Matt wouldn't want me beating myself up and blaming myself for any of it. Even if I had been at fault, he wouldn't want me beating up on myself. He was always generous like that.'

For a fraction of a second something in Elodie's eyes lightened. In a heartbeat, it was gone again. He despaired that anything he said would touch her.

'He wouldn't want you miring yourself in all of this bitterness and anger either.'

'You have no idea what he'd want!'

'Not true,' he said slowly. And in some fundamental way that gave him back his brother. 'Matt would want me to support you in any and every way I could. He'd want me to have a good relationship with Oliver. And this will sound harsh when I don't want it to but, Elodie, Oliver deserves better.'

Her quick intake of breath speared into his heart. 'How dare you?' Her whisper was hoarse. 'I love my son.'

'I know you do, but Oliver deserves to have all of you, not half of you.'

She backed away from him, shaking her head.

'Do you want to know what it's like beyond the anger and bitterness?'

She stared, swallowed and glanced away. 'How?'

'It's not much different in some ways. I miss Matt every single day. So much, sometimes it's like there's a hole inside me.'

She pressed a hand to her mouth.

'But letting go of my guilt and anger—at myself and the universe—has forced me to accept that Matt is really gone for good.'

She stiffened.

'It doesn't matter how much I don't want that to be true. It's a fact. Matt isn't coming back.'

Her bottom lip wobbled.

'In its place I've been remembering some of the good times we had—some big, some small. They pop into my mind when I'm least expecting it. Like the week Gran took us on a yachting holiday to the Lake District. We were ten and twelve. It was magic.' He couldn't help smiling at the memory. 'Matt's excitement when he got into his dream college at Cambridge.' He waited for her to meet his eyes. 'The tone of his voice when he told me he'd met the girl he was going to marry.'

Elodie's shoulders started to shake and he did what he should've done nine months ago. He pulled her against his chest and held her as she cried out her grief and her pain.

Cleo stared at Jude sleeping. His face at rest looked more youthful, more at peace. She resisted the urge to reach across and press her lips to his. These last few days had been idyllic. She still couldn't believe that from so much disaster she'd found so much *joy*.

The thought had her swallowing. This was a temporary refuge. She couldn't forget that. She and Jude were finding temporary consolation in each other, nothing more. They'd become friends and then lovers. The former would hopefully endure, but the latter had an end date. In six days' time, she'd return to London and be the model of propriety at her sister's wedding.

Six days? She glanced at Jude again. Would she get her fill of this man in that time? Together they'd scaled heights she hadn't known existed. And yet it hadn't taken the edge off her hunger, or his.

The thought of leaving him… An ache gripped her chest. Slipping out of bed, she padded through to her own bedroom and changed into a pair of jogging bottoms. Jude considered love an exercise in *deception, disillusion and despair*. He had no interest in anything long-term. She had to respect that.

And anything beyond a clandestine affair was out of the question. For pity's sake, he was a hundred times more high-profile than any of her previous boyfriends. Think of the media frenzy. If their names were linked, it would create *so* much tabloid speculation. Exhaustion swept through her. She was tired of being in the limelight, tired of the derogatory innuendos, tired of no one taking her seriously.

She dragged on her trainers and pulled the laces tight. She'd sworn to Margot she'd fly under the radar. She *would* keep her promise. She simply needed a moment to get her scattered emotions back under control. They were running high today, which was to be expected. Letting herself outside, she set off around the massive gardens at a fast clip, the air icy in her lungs.

Jude met her on the terrace on her return. He smiled, but his gaze searched her face. 'You had the energy for a run?'

She shrugged. 'A necessity. Your chef is a gem, and I've been indulging a little too much.'

'Come and have breakfast. You can shower later. Elodie won't mind.'

He'd told her about his conversation with Elodie. His courage in baring himself to the other woman had left her speechless. The gulf had been breached, though, and both Jude and Elodie were doing their best to mend their relationship. She didn't doubt there'd be rocky times ahead, but nor did she doubt their ability to get through them. She'd been so happy for him.

'It's due to you,' he'd told her.

'Nonsense!'

'I've seen how fearless you've been in mending your relationship with Margot. I've seen how determined you are to not let her down—the lengths you've gone to and the sacrifices you've made.'

'She's my sister,' she'd said, as if that explained it all.

'*Exactly.* You refuse to let your own hurt or resentment or guilt stop you from doing what you can to fix things. Even when that turns your life upside down. Even when the demands made on you aren't reasonable. You've done it gladly, without complaint. Me? I just went into hiding.'

'You were grieving.' In his shoes, she'd have travelled those same depths of despair. 'You needed time, and now you've had it you're seeing what you need to do, and you're doing it. You should be proud of yourself.'

She'd kissed him then and there hadn't been talking for a very long time.

Afterwards, when she'd been luxuriating in a golden glow of contentment, Jude had turned his head on the pillow. 'Meeting you has changed my life, Cleo. For the better.'

She'd had to blink away tears. She'd nestled against his side and pressed a hand over his heart. 'Ditto, Jude.'

She followed him through to the dining room now, and Elodie's brows shot up when she saw Cleo's running gear. 'A run? Is it not freezing outside? Did not you and Jude use the indoor gym earlier in the week?'

'It was *bracing.* And I like the fresh air.' She grinned. 'I'm also aware I'll be walking down the aisle in a bridesmaid's dress in a week and I want to fit into it.'

Elodie laughed, but was it Cleo's imagination or had Jude's eyes clouded over at the reminder she wouldn't be here this time next week? She shook off the thought—definitely her imagination.

She glanced up a short while later to find him frowning at the way she picked at an omelette. She forced herself to lift a morsel to her lips and make noises of approval.

His frown deepened. 'Is something wrong?'

Elodie became instantly alert then too. Cleo abandoned her cutlery and willed the tears away. 'It's Saturday.'

They both nodded.

She tried to smile, but the sudden concern that flickered across Elodie's face, and the way Jude's

brows lowered, made her think she hadn't suc-
ceeded. 'It's Margot's hen night tonight and...'
She trailed off with a shrug. She ought to be there.

Jude and Elodie threw her a party. Jude surprised
her with a designer dress in hot pink that he'd had
specially delivered. Fun and flirty, it fitted like
a dream and made her feel like a princess. And
the relatives who'd travelled to the château for
the weekend joined in the festivities with gusto.

The château's chef excelled herself. There were
delicious platters of canapés—clever things made
with prawns, bacon and asparagus—exotic sal-
ads and cold meats. Sweets included tiny crème
brûlées in shot glasses and mini chocolate eclairs.
There was non-alcoholic fizz to wash it all down.

There were party games that had everyone
laughing, and dancing under the lights of a
disco ball. Everyone wanted to dance with her,
and made the most delicious fuss. Jude's family
were warm and loving with the same bone-deep
decency that ran in Jude's veins. Their enjoyment
wasn't feigned, and it made Cleo realise what she
lacked in her own life—a sense of belonging, a
place where she could be herself and not always
be so guarded and on her best behaviour.

'Would you like to record a message for the
bride?' Jude asked later in the evening.

'Yes, please!' She handed him her phone to do
the recording.

The volume of the music was turned down, though the disco ball continued to flash, and she stood in front of the crowd who all cheered and waved from behind her.

'Margot, I so wish I could be celebrating with you tonight. I hope you're having the most wonderful time and are looking forward to marrying the man of your dreams next weekend. You've been the best sister a girl could ever hope for and I'm lucky to have you in my life. Because I can't be there with you tonight, I'm celebrating you here with my new friends.' She raised her glass. 'To Margot!'

'To Margot!' everyone cried behind her, raising their glasses.

She blew Margot a kiss and Jude stopped the video. She immediately sent it and crossed her fingers that Margot would send her a reply—a happy reply.

An hour later, just as the party was winding up, her phone vibrated in her pocket: a text from Margot. Her heart picked up speed.

What is your gratitude list today?

Another text pinged.

Top of my list is my message from you. xx

'Everything okay?'

Jude watched her with bright intent and she doubted she could've blinked the tears from her eyes or stopped her smile—not even if there'd been a photographer's camera trained on her. 'From Margot.'

She held out her phone so he could read the text, her breath doing a funny little stutter in her throat when a grin spread across his stern features. Giving a whoop, he picked her up and swung her round, and for the briefest of moments it felt as if everything in her world had aligned.

'Happy?' he demanded, setting her on her feet again.

'Over the moon!' A moment later, she murmured, 'People are staring.' Though they were staring at him, not her—and in bemusement, not disapproval.

'Don't care.'

And why should he? These people, his family, were people he could trust. They'd accept him for who and what he was.

*You can trust your family too.*

*Not like this.*

*Whose fault is that?*

She pushed the thought away. She'd made things right between Margot and her again, which meant they'd be okay again between Cleo and her father. She'd be careful not to create more drama or scandal and everything would be just fine.

She clasped her phone to her chest. 'Thank you,

Jude. Not just for this party, but for everything. For helping me save the day.'

'You saved the day yourself, Cleo. I just gave you a place to hide.'

'You came to my rescue more times than I can count. You let me stowaway on your boat.'

'Grudgingly.' He grimaced.

'You whisked me away to the French Riviera when it became clear journalists were on our tails.'

He shrugged, as if that was nothing.

'And then you brought me here because I couldn't relax with all of those darn helicopters.'

He gazed around, his face softening. 'It's good to be back.' He looked more content than she'd seen him.

And, just like that, every atom flooded with awareness: for the strong, lean lines of Jude's body that felt like silken steel beneath her fingertips; for firm lips that could be as gentle as a summer breeze through the fronds of a weeping willow, or as demanding as a surging tide; for the feel of his body moving against hers, as if the fact of them becoming lovers had always been inevitable. As if there were molecules in him and her that otherwise would've always remained dormant.

*Dangerous*, a voice whispered through her.

'This hasn't been one-sided, Cleo. If it weren't for you...'

His words petered out when he registered her desire and need. She couldn't hide it. Her body pulsed with it, on fire with an urgency she couldn't explain. The darkening of his eyes and the quickening of the pulse at his throat told her he felt the same.

'Party's breaking up.'

His hoarse whisper rasped across her skin. 'Do you think that means it'd be okay if we slipped away?' she whispered.

Taking her hand, he pulled her from the room.

'They're all going to know.' Her heart pounded in her throat. 'That was hardly discreet.'

'I don't care.'

Then she wouldn't either.

The moment they reached their suite, she slammed the door behind them and backed him up against it. Stretching up on tiptoe, she pressed her lips to the spot where his pulse pounded in his throat, lathing it with her tongue and drinking in the scent of him—all spice, fresh mint and warm musk, a heady combination that made her head spin.

As did the sound of air hissing from his lungs and the touch of his fingers at her waist.

'I wanted to do that all night,' she said, pressing a series of kisses along his jaw towards that beautiful, beguiling mouth.

'Want to know what I've wanted to do?'

He'd eased back a fraction so she'd have to

stand higher on tiptoe to reach his lips, but his hands tightened on her waist and she couldn't move. She nodded.

He lifted the hem of her skirt in one motion until it was hitched around her waist, the move shockingly brazen and shockingly seductive. In a flash of movement, he whirled them around so it was her back pressed against the door. His fingers slid beneath the lace of her panties with a wicked intimacy—his fingers unapologetically bold and searching. She gave a shocked moan of need, her head lolling back against the door.

He swore softly in French, making her toes curl. 'I touch you like this…' that finger moved against her with merciless thoroughness that made her legs tremble '…and I'm in danger of losing control.'

'Please…lose…control.' Each word was ground out—a gasp and a plea.

'It's why I've taken to carrying condoms with me wherever we go.' He tore the corner of a foil packet with his teeth.

Cleo had given up speaking, too busy fumbling with his belt and then the zip of his trousers. He sheathed himself in the condom and lifted her. She wrapped her legs around his waist and he entered her in a smooth motion that filled her body, making her mindless, spiralling her to another place—a place of pleasure and delight where they both rode wave upon wave of pleasure that lasted forever.

She came back to herself to find Jude resting his forehead on the door beside her. Her arms were looped round his neck and her legs dangled loosely round his hips. Turning her head, she pressed a kiss to his neck. Very gently, he eased away and let her slide down until her feet touched the floor.

'I think I might've screamed loud enough for them to have heard me back in England.' She'd never realised she could be so vocal.

'I couldn't hear you over the noise I was making.'

He grinned. She grinned.

'Don't worry, Cinderella, the castle walls are thick.'

They made love again. Of course they did.

Afterwards Cleo watched as the light outside the window began to filter into the room while Jude slept beside her. She'd never had such a generous lover. She hadn't known that making love could be this good. But she was starting to feel as if it meant more to her than it should. She could feel herself wanting to plan a future with Jude.

She needed to knock that on the head because it simply wasn't going to happen. He'd warned her that he didn't do long-term. And last night she'd fully reconnected with Margot at last. Margot had finally forgiven her. She couldn't do anything to risk upsetting that balance. Acid burned her stomach—which another disastrous love affair with another high-profile man would absolutely do.

Silently she slid from Jude's bed and made her way to her own room to slide between smooth sheets that felt too crisp and cold.

'You returned to your own room this morning.'

Jude watched Cleo's face closely as she sipped her tea. The staff brought a pot of tea into the library at ten-thirty every morning. It was where he and Cleo had taken to working. Often an hour or more would go by without them speaking, both immersed in their work—she with her website designs and he writing the third book of his trilogy.

Dammed for so long, the words now flowed with a speed he could barely keep up with. He couldn't explain how, but writing again made him feel strong—gave him the resources to deal with other tougher things.

He couldn't stop thinking about Cleo's suggestion to change the internal structure of Giroux Holdings. He'd started researching what it would involve and had made a list of family members to approach. It had filled him with a new sense of purpose and a new optimism for the future.

Her gaze skittered away from his now. 'I was feeling a bit restless. I didn't want to disturb you.'

His heart sank. It was a lie—or at least not the

full truth. He understood it, though. Their love-making had taken on a new edge—had become something deeper, both fiercer and more tender somehow. It had filled him with exhilaration. But, staring at Cleo's face now, he realised the other side of that equation.

'What?'

He blinked to find her frowning at him.

'You've turned grim,' she said.

'I didn't mean to. I just…' Moving from his desk and pouring himself a tea, he forced himself to sit in his usual spot on the sofa beside her, careful to keep some space between them.

'You just…what?'

'I just realised what you're doing. You're trying to create some distance between us, and I can see the wisdom in that.' Neither of them had made promises. Neither of them was looking for a relationship.

'Last night we were indiscreet.' The way they'd beaten a hasty retreat from the party wouldn't have gone unnoticed. In the cold light of morning, did Cleo regret that? Was she worried rumours would reach the tabloids? 'I promise you can trust my family, *and* the staff here. No word of this will reach outside ears.'

She turned back so fast, tea sloshed in her saucer. 'I trust you and them.' Setting her teacup onto the coffee table, she turned to him more fully. 'I love making love with you, Jude, but we were clear from the beginning about not making any kind of commitment to one another. We always knew that our...*amour*...'

His lips twitched at the quaintness of the word on her lips. She half-smiled too, and he found an odd comfort in that. 'We always knew our *liaison* had an end date,' he finished for her.

'Yes.'

She'd be returning to England on Friday—in five days' time, he realised with a jolt. 'You're worried I'll read more into our affair than I should.' As the words left his mouth, he wondered if she had every right to worry.

'I want to make sure *I* don't start reading more into it.'

Her hands twisted and it was all he could do not to lean over and cover them with his own.

'My past has proved that me rushing headlong into things without thinking is a recipe for disaster.'

And they had rushed headlong into their affair. He didn't regret it, but she was right: it was time to be sensible. It was time to remember the boundaries they'd set.

'Now that Margot has forgiven me, I can't afford to do anything to ruin that.'

His jaw clenched. 'You should live your life to please yourself, Cleo, not to make your sister and father happy.'

She reared back, as if he'd slapped her. 'It just

so happens that those things are inextricably en-twined. And you'd be lying if you said it wasn't the same for you.'

That was true, but it seemed to him that it was Cleo who made all the sacrifices and compro-mises in her relationship with her family, while Margot and their father made none. But it was none of his business and he had no right to criti-cise. He nodded. 'You're right.'

'I just want to get my life back on track.' She rolled her eyes. 'And *never* appear on the front page of a newspaper again.'

And being linked with him would mean living her life in the spotlight, which was everything she didn't want.

'Are you angry?'

He stared at her, shocked she could think such a thing. 'No! I'm thinking how right you are and how wise you're being. We didn't make promises for very good reasons.' His chest grew heavy as the weight of those reasons pressed down on him. 'My and Elodie's relationship has started to mend, but the equilibrium is...'

'Delicate?'

*Exactly.* It'd be cruel to flaunt any sort of ro-mantic happiness in front of her when she was grieving for Matt. Had Elodie witnessed Cleo's and his exit from the party last night? He scanned his memory, sagging when he realised she'd excused herself earlier. But she'd probably hear the speculations of all those who'd been present.

He squared his shoulders. She wouldn't hear any more, though; he'd make sure of it. He glanced back at Cleo. 'I have so much I need to do, so much to accomplish. It deserves my best efforts.'

She nodded her understanding and drew closer. 'Okay, this is what we're going to do: for the next five days, we're going to be discreet.'

She was gifting him the next five days!

She tapped his chest. '*Seriously* discreet.'

Taking her face in his hands, he kissed her. 'Deal.'

# CHAPTER ELEVEN

EVERY DAY CLEO'S departure grew closer, the darker Jude's world became. Was it because it meant the adventure would end? He'd never felt more alive than he had in these last two-and-a-half weeks.

She'd helped him see things so differently. Was he concerned they'd go back to the way they'd been? Was he worried about taking up the mantle as head of the family, or finishing the current book?

It all fell into place for him on Thursday afternoon. He couldn't let Cleo go. He'd fallen in love with her. Despite his best efforts, despite believing love an exercise in deception, disillusion and despair.

The thing was, Cleo had never deceived him. She'd eased the despair of his grief…and she'd turned his disillusion into wonder, and had made him see a world worth fighting for. His scowling and grumpiness had been no match for her teasing, her laughter or her frank confessions. And the thought of her leaving...

Of course she needed to go to her sister's wedding. But then *she had to come back*. Their attraction had taken them both off-guard. Was it out of the realms of possibility that love could take her by surprise as well?

She *liked* him. And the way she made love with him that evening made him dare hope.

Lying in bed afterwards, trailing his hand idly over the soft skin of her back, he wanted this forever. 'Cleo, is it really outside the realms of possibility that after Margot's wedding we couldn't see each other again?'

'What do you mean?'

She looked warm and rumpled and utterly beautiful. 'You and I have always been honest with each other.' He frowned. 'Well, okay, I mightn't have told you who I was immediately.'

'We've always been honest about the things that mattered,' she agreed, sliding her hand into his.

Generous—that was Cleo. He pulled in a breath. 'Which is why I want to be honest with you now.'

Blinking, she sat up, drawing the sheet with her. 'Okay.'

He sat up too. 'I'd like to see you again.'

Something in her face softened. 'Oh, Jude. I've loved the time I've spent with you.'

*Loved.* She used the word *loved.*

But then she shook her head. 'I don't think that's a good idea.'

Was that because she thought he was toying with her...wasn't serious? 'Would it make any difference if I told you I've fallen in love with you?'

Her jaw dropped. She stared as if she hadn't heard him right.

He rolled his shoulders. 'I didn't mean for it to happen. It wasn't part of my plan. But I have and...' He petered off as he recognised the emotion dawning in her eyes: horror.

Backing away, she scrambled out of bed and thrust her arms into her robe, tying it tightly at her waist before turning to face him. 'You said your heart was safe! You told me you wouldn't fall in love with me!'

'I didn't know I had!' The accusation in her tone stung. 'I realised this afternoon, which is why I'm telling you now.'

She raked both hands through her hair. 'This can't happen, Jude.'

Leaping out of bed, he hauled on a pair of boxers. 'Why not?'

'We had rules!'

'Which we both kept breaking.'

Her gaze caught on his chest and she swallowed.

'Why not?' he repeated. 'I know you want me.'

The expression in her eyes assured him of that. 'And I know you like me.'

'Of course I do! But attraction and like aren't...'

She broke off, and he went cold all over. Ice crawled across his scalp. He'd been reading too much into it all—her warmth, her generosity, her honesty—because it meant so much to him. And to imagine his world without her in it was unbearable.

'You do *not* need someone like me in your life, Jude. And neither does your family. Believe me, I am not *"on brand".* She made quote marks in the air.

*What the hell...?*

'Once the papers get wind of the story—' she gestured between them '—and things get real, you'd see that too.'

Did she think he'd abandon her?

'And what about *my* family, Jude? My notoriety reflects on them. It impacts their careers. They don't deserve to have their colleagues and friends whispering behind their backs every time my life is splashed across the papers. They deserve better than that. They deserve *better* from me.'

All his wealth and the power of his family name wouldn't be able to prevent the story from hitting the headlines once he and Cleo were linked. It was everything she didn't want; she'd told him that repeatedly. What part of that hadn't he heard and heeded?

'My family deserve me to lay low for a while.' She dragged in a breath. 'They deserve me to be whole and happy for them.'

He rocked back on his heels. He clearly wasn't part of a future where she saw herself as either whole or happy. His mouth tasted of ashes.

Her chin wobbled. 'I'd give a thousand worlds not to have hurt you—'

'I'm sorry I raised the topic,' he cut in. 'I shouldn't have said anything.' He could see that now.

Her knuckles turned white from where they gripped the front of her robe. 'I'm sorry, Jude,' she whispered.

She left, closing his bedroom door softly behind her. It felt as if every light in the world had gone out.

He drove her to the airport the following afternoon. What little conversation they had, they kept practical.

'Has your father organised a car for you at the other end?'

'Yes.'

'I've arranged a contact to take you to the first-class lounge.'

'That's very kind. Thank you.'

Her hands twisted in her lap. She bit her lip and stared out of the window. Her misery washed over him in waves. He should never have burdened her with his declaration last night. If he'd been thinking with any logic at all, he'd have waited until after the wedding—waited until she'd felt secure again. Then he could've orchestrated a meeting and they could've taken it from there. Instead, he'd told her he loved her, and now the guilt at being unable to return his feelings was eating her alive. For God's sake, he knew how beholden she felt to him!

He pulled the car into a space at Departures. 'Cleo, I want you to understand that knowing you has made my life better. I also want you to know that I'm going to be fine.'

She swallowed. 'Of course you are.'

'I'm disappointed, but…' He shrugged. 'I've much to keep me busy.'

She turned to him. 'I can't thank you enough for everything you've done.'

'Then don't. It's been a pleasure.'

Her gaze met his and she nodded, then she gestured out of the window. 'Don't come in with me. It'll be better this way.'

He wanted to argue, but didn't. 'Let me text my contact to say we're here. He'll take you the back ways the media don't know about.' He sent the text. The silence between them stretched. He found his fingers going to his pocket, reaching for her sunglasses as if they were a talisman.

'You know—' he held them up '—you never did tell me what the story was with these.'

She glanced at them and then smiled, truly smiled. His heart started pounding like a wild thing.

'They were my mother's.'

His jaw dropped. Her *mother's*?

'She loved those sunglasses; she took them everywhere. When she died, I asked for them. They've been my most treasured possession ever since.'

He thrust them at her, horror filling his belly. 'You must take them back!' He couldn't deprive her of her mother's sunglasses. He'd have never made that deal if he'd known…

She shook her head. 'She'd have been so proud of me for the deal I made with you, Jude. And that means more to me than anything.' Reaching out, she curled his fingers back around the sunglasses, touching her other hand to her heart. 'I carry my mother with me wherever I go. I don't need a pair of sunglasses to remind me of that, not any more. Keep them. Use them and enjoy them, and remember how you once helped a silly girl out of a pickle—that will make me happy.'

He put them back in his pocket. He'd treasure them forever.

Jude's contact appeared and opened Cleo's door. 'I will be pleased to be of service to any friend of Monsieur Blackwood.'

Cleo smiled her thanks, before holding her hand out to Jude. 'Thank you.'

He curved his fingers round her hand, fixing the feel of her in his mind for the very last time. 'It's been a pleasure knowing you, Cleo.'

He watched her until she disappeared from view, the weight bearing down on his chest growing heavier and heavier.

Elodie took one look at Jude's face when he returned, and she lifted the coffee pot in a silent question. He shook his head.

She set it back down. 'Did Cleo get off without drama?'

'Yes.'

'She must be excited about the wedding.'

'Yes.'

He ached to talk about her. In equal measure he ached not to talk about her. 'Excuse me, Elodie, I have some calls to make.' Turning on his heel, he left the room.

It was just Elodie and him for dinner that evening. Unusual for a Friday night, but there was a glittering black-tie affair in the city that many of the extended clan were attending. Elodie cut into her perfectly cooked chicken breast before glancing across at him. 'When is Cleo to return?'

He kept his gaze on his food. 'She isn't returning, Elodie. Our business here is complete.'

Her cutlery clattered to her plate. 'That's nonsense!'

Elodie's lips had pinched into a tight line and his throat went dry. 'Why?'

'Anyone with eyes in their head can see the two of you have feelings for one another.'

All of this time he'd thought they'd been discreet… He rubbed a hand over his face. 'You must hate me.'

'Hate you? *Why?*' She blinked at whatever she saw in his face. 'Because I lost my love, you are therefore not allowed your love? Is that what you think?' When he remained silent, she slammed her hands on the table. 'Do you think me so ungenerous?'

'No! I just…'

'Did it not occur to you that seeing the people around me fall in love and find happiness might be a form of consolation?'

He closed his eyes and let out a breath. 'I might be in love with Cleo, Elodie, but she's not in love with me.'

Elodie gave an undignified snort. 'You did not see her face when she was telling me what a heroic Galahad you had been, saving her from all the journalists. You did not see how her eyes softened when she said how kind you had been to her.'

'And you didn't see her face when she told me she doesn't want the complication of a relationship with someone as high-profile as me.'

Her eyes narrowed. 'Did she tell you she did not love you?'

'Yes.'

'Did she say those actual words?'

He frowned. She'd certainly implied it.

'Tell me what she said, exactly—because I do not believe she does not love you.'

He told her as much as he had the heart to.

Elodie folded her arms. 'She told you what you needed and she told you what her family needed. She did *not* tell you she didn't love you.'

'That's semantics.'

'She is afraid she cannot fit into our world. She is afraid of letting you down. She is afraid of letting her sister and her father down. She is doing what she thinks is the best thing for everyone.'

*She*… His frown deepened and his mind raced.

Her panic when he'd said he'd loved her; the expression on her face at the airport; the fact she'd given him her mother's sunglasses: had all that meant something after all?

*Wishful thinking.*

'It seems to me that Cleo fights for everyone else's happiness.' Elodie glared at him. 'But nobody seems to be fighting for Cleo.'

He shot to his feet, his hands clenching and unclenching. Elodie was right. He hadn't fought for Cleo. He'd made his declaration, she'd panicked and he'd retreated into his shell like a scared little hermit crab. He'd let Cleo walk away without a murmur of protest. He hadn't told her that he loved her again. He hadn't told her that, if she changed her mind, to call him. He hadn't told her he'd be there if she ever needed him.

What he'd told her was that he'd be okay. As if losing her hadn't shattered his world. As if his broken heart was a small thing easily recovered from. Cleo might not love him, but she deserved a man who would fight for her. And, if there was the slightest chance of winning her love, he'd fight with everything he had.

Cleo arrived at the Dorchester under the cover of darkness and was whisked straight up to a suite of rooms her father had organised for the bride and her attendant.

Other than the butler on hand to ensure she had all that she needed, the suite was empty. 'Your things arrived earlier, Ms Milne, and have been unpacked.' She handed her a letter. 'Your sister asked that I give you this.'

Cleo took the letter. 'Thank you.' Where was everyone?

'Dinner has been ordered for you for seven-thirty.'

Would Margot and her father be joining her then?

'If you need anything, please ring.' The butler gestured towards the phone and Cleo managed a polite smile before the other woman left. She felt like a robot. Ever since she'd walked away from Jude, she'd felt like half a person.

It had taken all her strength to force herself out of the car and to walk away from him this afternoon. The real reason she hadn't wanted him to come into the airport with her was that she hadn't been sure her resolve would hold. She had been afraid she'd weaken and tell him she loved him too.

But what had loving her given anyone? Nothing but headaches and heartache. Jude didn't need a mess like her in his life. He'd been through enough. He needed all his energy and resources to take his place as the head of the Giroux family. She swallowed. He'd forget about her soon enough.

Which was just as well, because with her on his arm he'd be nothing more than a laughing stock. He deserved better. He deserved the best.

She rubbed a hand across her chest, trying to ease the ache there. Nor could she let her sister down again. She hungered to make Margot and their father proud of her. And she would! Regardless of what it cost her.

She gritted her teeth. Staring at Hyde Park through the French doors, she rested her shoulder against the door frame and tore open Margot's letter.

*Cleo,*
*Dad and I think it's best if you spend the night in the hotel suite where journalists can't get to you, while I spend the night at the family home. We'll arrive at the hotel at ten a.m. on the dot, as will the hairdressers and make-up artists, along with the seamstress, in case last-minute alterations are necessary.*
*Do not step foot outside your room. Do you hear me? Do not mess this up for me. If you do—*

That last half-sentence had been left unfinished and the words had been crossed out, but they blazed off the page like a threat.

*I will see you tomorrow.*

It was signed *M*—no love, no kisses, no thank you. Just '*do not mess this up for me*'.

The letter dropped from her nerveless fingers and floated to the floor. 'The seamstress won't be necessary,' she whispered.

Cleo gazed in the mirror the next morning and hoped the make-up artist was a magician. She'd barely slept a wink, and hadn't touched her food last night or this morning. She looked as lacklustre as she felt.

She practised a smile, and then another one, because the first was so appalling. She *wouldn't* ruin Margot's big day. But a growing sense of disquiet had been building inside her since reading Margot's letter. She'd thought Margot had forgiven her. She'd thought things were right between them again. She'd done everything that Margot had asked of her—*everything*.

There was a slim chance that Margot had turned into a panic-stricken Bridezilla, but the more Cleo thought about it the less likely that seemed. For heaven's sake, Margot had trained as an international lawyer and was embarking on a political career. The one thing Margot *did* have was nerves of steel. And yet Margot continued to avoid her.

Cleo made herself smile in the mirror again and, while the smile was better, the tears that filled her eyes completely ruined the effect.

She forced them down. She suspected she knew why Margot was avoiding her and it had nausea churning in her stomach. She flashed back to New Year's Eve, once again feeling the impact of her fist colliding with Clay's jaw after those dreadful words had left his mouth. If what he'd said hadn't been a pack of lies…

A knock on the door had her straightening. Margot and Dad were ten minutes early. *Smile*, she silently ordered herself as she rushed out of the *en suite* and through the bedroom to fling open the door . 'Margot, I—'

She stopped dead, her mouth working, but not a single syllable emerging.

*Jude! Jude* stood on the other side of the door, looking grumpy, dishevelled and utterly wonderful and she drank him in with a greedy thirst. His scowl deepened. 'Can I come in?'

Closing a hand round one strong forearm, she hauled him inside, glancing outside the corridor to make sure it was empty before slamming the door shut. Her fingers tingled from where she'd touched him. She had to fight the urge to fling herself into his arms.

'Jude! What are you doing here?'

'I needed to see you. I forgot to ask you something.'

The expression in his eyes turned her insides to mush. She did everything she could to harden her heart. 'You can't stay.'

*Oh, God! Margot and Dad would be here any moment.* If they found Jude here… Her heart stuttered. They'd think she'd reverted to type. That she'd been partying and drinking. They'd believe the lies the newspapers had printed about her. Their smiles would slip, their mouths would twist, a cynical disillusion would spread across their faces. Worst of all, it would cast a shadow and a stain on Margot's day that could never be erased.

'There's something I need to ask you, Cleo.'

She barely heard him. Her heart fluttered too fast, like the wings of a hummingbird. Everything was unravelling.

Jude's hands curved around her shoulders. 'Cleo, I need to know—'

A knock on the door and Margot's, 'Cleo?' had her wanting to cry.

Jude stared at the door. His eyes widened. 'I thought there would be time before the wedding prep took over.' He kept his voice low. 'The wedding isn't till four o'clock.'

Seizing the front of his shirt, she shook him. 'They can *not* find you here.'

He spread his hands in a gesture that said 'what the hell do you want me to do?'

She pushed him into her bedroom. *'Hide.'*

'Where?'

'The *en suite*, wardrobe, under the bed... I don't care!' Hopefully there'd be a chance to sneak him out when no one was looking.

Another knock came. 'Cleo!' Margot sounded impatient.

'Coming!' She pointed a warning finger at Jude as she pulled the bedroom door closed, then rushed to answer the door. Her father and Margot stood on the threshold, thankfully alone. The army of hairdressers, make-up artists and dressers were yet to arrive.

They both gave her perfunctory kisses on the cheek—no hugs, no warm words.

*Why had Jude come?*

'I was starting to wonder if you were here.' Margot's ash-blonde hair swung in a shiny curtain as she moved past.

'Of course I'm here. I received my orders and have been following them like a good soldier.' She'd meant to say the words lightly, but they held an edge that made her wince internally.

Margot turned with stricken eyes—as if Cleo had plunged a knife into her heart. Cleo made herself smile and shrug. 'I was in the bathroom, that's all. Now, should I order tea to be sent up? Or maybe you'd like a glass of fizz instead?'

Was it her imagination or did Margot look a little green?

*Did you really just order Jude to hide?*

Her father strode to the phone and requested both tea and champagne to be sent up, before settling on one of the sofas. Cleo couldn't drag her gaze from her sister's. Margot swallowed. 'I trust you had a pleasant night?'

She'd spent fewer more miserable nights in her life. She'd missed Jude with an ache that had made her chest cramp. She'd missed Margot and the fun of the night before the wedding. She'd missed their mother. *Everything* had felt wrong.

'Yes, thank you.'

Margot's and her gazes remained locked. She could tell Margot wanted to break the contact, but couldn't. She recognised some of the emotions churning in the amber brown of her sister's eyes and for a moment she wanted to cry. Clay's ugly words went round and round in her mind.

'Cleo,' Michael Milne started, oblivious to the silent battle going on between his daughters, 'I wanted to say how impressed I am. You've handled yourself extremely well over the last two-and-a-half weeks.'

That had Margot swinging around. 'No thanks to you! I still can't believe you turned her out of the family home.'

Cleo smiled then because she knew in that moment, despite her fears, that she hadn't lost her sister. 'Clay told me you and he had kissed.' The words blurted from her. She wished she'd found a way to say them with more grace, but the air needed to be cleared.

Margot turned back, her pallor making Cleo wince. Their father rose to his feet.

'He put it far more crudely than that—called you something dreadful. And, before I'd even realised it, I'd hit him. Over the years I've heard a lot of bad things said about you, Dad, because of the politician thing, but I'd never heard anyone say anything awful about you, Margot. If you're going to be a politician, I'm going to need to work on that. I can't go around beating up everyone who says something mean.'

Margot's knuckles turned white where she gripped them in front of her. 'Cleo, I—'

'I didn't believe it at first. The penny only dropped because of the way you've continued to avoid me. I—'

'You kissed your sister's boyfriend?' Michael suddenly roared.

'Don't you start!' Cleo rounded on him. 'Margot has always tried to be perfect to make up to the both of us for losing Mum.'

He blinked.

'She looked after me when you closed yourself off, but who looked after her, huh? Not once has she ever rebelled. You've absolutely no right to judge her.'

His jaw slackened.

Grabbing Margot's hands, she squeezed them hard. 'The thing is, I don't care if it *is* true. You could do something a hundred times worse and I'd still forgive you. Look at all I put you through, and yet you still stood by me.'

Margot's face crumpled. 'I'm so sorry, Cleo. *So* sorry. I've never been more ashamed of myself. I—'

A knock sounded: the tea and champagne. Cleo gestured for it to be placed on the sideboard.

*What was Jude doing here?*

Only when they were alone again did she speak. 'I was never in love with Clay. You knew that.' She frowned. 'Why did you talk me out of breaking up with him?'

'I felt so guilty about what had happened. I

blamed myself and that stupid kiss for your changing feelings for him. I was worried I'd wrecked things for you.'

'So you wanted me to give it another chance?'

'I just wanted you to be sure. The thing is, Clay really did love you. I felt a bit sorry for him.'

It was Cleo's turn to blink.

'I think it's why he kissed me—he was searching for comfort from someone he associated with you. It's not really an excuse, but...'

But it was a human thing to do.

*Did you really just order Jude to hide?*

She glanced at her father and gestured to the tea things. 'Do you want to play Mother?'

He moved across and poured the tea.

'As for me...' Margot stared down at her hands before meeting Cleo's eyes once more. 'I was having one of the worst weeks of my life. A parliamentary paper I'd spent months working on was sent back to the drawing board and the party had decided not to approve my nomination just yet.'

*They'd what?* 'But—'

'They changed their minds a few days later, but...'

She nodded to let Margot know she understood.

'Worse than that, though, Brett and I had a huge fight. We never fight, and it was unexpectedly fierce.' She grimaced. 'He made his excuses and didn't come to Dad's sixtieth birthday party.'

*Ah, so that's why Brett hadn't been there.*

'I thought we were over. You and a few of the other girls were talking about what we should do for my hen night and I didn't have the heart to take part, so I drifted off. I found myself alone with Clay in the library. It was obvious he felt a bit left out and...'

She shrugged, the skin at the corners of her eyes drawing tight. 'It was stupid. But for that brief moment we felt like two lost souls and we turned to each other for solace. We sprang apart a moment later, both utterly appalled.'

Cleo's heart burned for her sister, and a little bit for Clay too. Pulling in a breath, she pressed her hands together. 'I need to check—are you sure you want to marry Brett?'

Margot stiffened.

'And, while we're talking so frankly, do you truly want to be a politician or are you doing that to make Dad happy?'

From the corner of her eye, she saw her dad's gaze sharpen.

'Yes, and yes. I told Brett about what had happened between me and Clay. I couldn't lie to him. He was hurt, but was mature enough to point out that we hadn't made any formal vows to each other at that point. He was ridiculously understanding. He still wants to marry me, and he knows I love him.'

Cleo sagged.

'I'm the luckiest woman in the world.' Margot's

smile told them she meant it. 'And I do want to be a politician, Cleo. I promise you I do. I want to make a difference, and it feels like the right platform to do that.'

Their father sagged then too.

Cleo clapped her hands. 'Look, we're all adults and it's time to start acting like it. We can't keep playing the same roles we have since Mum died.'

'Agreed,' Margot said.

Her father nodded. She pointed a finger at him. 'You need to be more present.' She turned to Margot. 'You need to stop trying to be perfect. And I—' she slapped a hand on her chest '—need to stop appearing in the papers. I know the tabloids love labelling me a wild child, but I need to stop providing them with fodder!'

Her father frowned. 'But the reason you landed on the front page this time was…due to someone else's bad behaviour.' His frown deepened. 'And the time before that too.'

Margot stared at her. 'And the two times before that it was due to Ewan and… Oh, that pretty boy! What was his name?'

'Austin.' Cleo nodded and swallowed. 'I haven't been a wild child since I was twenty-two. It's just that no one wants to believe it.'

Margot took her hands. 'Then *you* don't need to change anything.'

'Yes, I do,' she said slowly, remembering something Jude had once said. 'I need to forgive myself for past mistakes and stop trying to win everyone's approval. I need to learn to be proud of myself instead.'

Proud of herself? She'd just pushed Jude—a man who'd proven himself a true friend, a man who'd told her *he loved her*—into the bedroom and ordered him to hide, as if he was something she was ashamed of.

Her stomach churned. What kind of person had she become? 'There's something I need to tell you both.' She pressed her hands together. 'Jude,' she called out, 'would you like to come out here?'

# CHAPTER TWELVE

JUDE STEPPED INTO the living room, his head spinning from all he'd overheard. The *someone* Clay had taunted Cleo with had been her *sister*?

Yet Cleo had still done Margot's bidding. She had done her utmost to ensure her wedding was everything she wanted. She'd effaced herself and put Margot's needs first. His heart pounded. Cleo loved so hard. If only he could convince her to love him just a little with that big heart of hers.

Cleo took his arm and faced her father and sister. 'This man helped me at his own personal expense when he didn't have to, just because he has a good heart. He went above and beyond.'

She dragged in a breath. 'He turned up here two minutes before you did and I panicked when you knocked, because I thought it might look bad if you found him here. I thought you'd be disappointed in me.'

She glanced up at Jude with burning eyes. 'That was an awful thing to do, Jude. I'm sorry.'

He shrugged. 'Apology accepted.'

'If it wasn't for this man, I'd have been plastered across all the newspapers *again*.'

Margot leapt forward and hugged him. 'Thank you for helping Cleo. I'm so grateful to you.' The warmth in her eyes had him understanding why Cleo loved her so much. She hugged Cleo too. 'I think we've been taking dysfunctional to a whole new level.'

'Nonsense.' Michael cleared his throat. 'This is just normal family...'

Cleo raised an eyebrow. 'Drama?'

'Dynamics?' Margot offered.

'Muddle.' He cleared his throat. 'When people care about each other they can get into the occasional muddle, that's all. And, while we're on the topic of being adults, Cleo, will you please introduce us to this young man?'

Cleo made the introductions.

Michael Milne's lips twisted, but there was a twinkle in his eyes. 'Now, in case you've forgotten, we're supposed to be having a wedding today, and the crew are impatiently waiting downstairs.' He held up his phone. 'I've been holding them off, but they're becoming increasingly frantic.'

Margot clasped Cleo's arm, her eyes going wide. 'I'm getting married!'

Cleo laughed. 'To the man of your dreams, remember?'

Margot's smile could've lit up an entire city block. Jude found himself grinning.

Margot wrung her hands. 'We have to get ready! I want it to be perfect!' She turned to Jude. 'Please come to my wedding.'

If it meant being near Cleo... 'I'd be honoured.'

'Come with me then, young man, and we'll get you sorted.' Michael clapped him on the shoulder.

Glancing back, he found Cleo watching him with eyes the colour of a still sea. Striding back, he squeezed her hand, the scent of pears engulfing him. 'Later,' he promised. He'd wait as long as he had to if there was the slightest chance of winning this woman's heart.

The wedding went without a hitch. The bride glowed while the groom couldn't wipe the grin from his face. Cleo, in a dress of dusky green that highlighted the colour of her eyes, was the picture of propriety.

Michael made a speech about how proud he was of his two daughters, how their happiness was his happiness, which barely left an eye in the room dry. The best man made a speech that had everyone laughing. And Cleo made a speech so heartfelt and sincere, it had a lump lodging in Jude's throat.

The cake was cut. The bridal waltz was danced. Jude's hands clenched as he watched the best man twirl a radiant Cleo across the dance floor. A young woman tapped his arm. 'We haven't been introduced, but Michael sent me over. He implied you'd be eager to dance with Cleo.'

*He had?*

'And as Cleo is dancing with my husband…'

*Excellent.*

'Shall we?'

He waltzed a direct path to Cleo. 'We're hoping to cut in.'

Cleo's eyes widened, but she moved into his arms without hesitation. 'Is it *later*?'

He nodded. Holding her so close, their bodies moving in harmony, had warmth encircling him and he closed his eyes to savour it.

'Why have we not waltzed before?' Cleo murmured, her left hand sliding further round his back so she could press herself closer.

Heat flooded his veins. 'Not much room for waltzing on a narrow boat.' And on the yacht they'd been too busy keeping their distance.

Mischievous eyes met his. 'It'd be fun to try, though.'

Images flooded his mind, making his nostrils flare.

'So…' She eased away a fraction. 'Are you enjoying the wedding?'

The wedding was nothing more than an interruption he had to endure before he could have Cleo to himself again. He hadn't prepared a speech, but…

Margot sidled up beside them. 'I seem to have torn the lace on my dress, Cleo. Can you pin it back up for me?'

Cleo stepped out of his arms with an apologetic wrinkle of her nose. 'Later is going to have to wait for a bit.'

He wanted to howl at the moon. He shrugged instead. 'For you, I'll wait as long as I have to.'

Her lovely lips parted, but then Margot tugged on her arm and Cleo moved away before he could kiss her which, despite the itch of impatience chafing through him, was probably for the best.

Cleo's heart pounded. What was Jude doing here? He'd said he'd wait as long as he had to, but... *why?* She'd already told him they couldn't be together. That had been hours ago. And, true to his word, he was still here—waiting.

And she loved it. *Loved him.* But she needed to fight that because the thought of letting him down at some future date and seeing his love turn to derision, realising she'd made his life worse instead of better... She didn't think she could bear it.

*What if you don't let him down?*

*Yeah, right, and pigs might fly.*

She did her best to focus on her bridesmaid duties. Margot and Brett were sent off with cheers and well wishes as they climbed into the white stretch limousine that would take them to a secret location. Cleo clasped her hands beneath her chin as the limousine pulled away. 'It was the most beautiful wedding.'

Her father rested an arm across her shoulders. 'It was a beautiful wedding, and your sister is a very happy woman. And, Cleo, I believe you will be too.'

She blinked when he took her arm and handed her inside a black cab that had drawn up behind the limo. 'Look after my girl, Jude.'

'I will.'

Jude slid in from the other side and her heart hammered, leapt and swooped. Her father pressed a kiss on her cheek, though she barely registered it, her mind too full of the man beside her. 'Give your dear old dad a call tomorrow, huh?' Dragging her gaze from Jude, she nodded.

The door closed, the cab pulled away and piercing blue eyes met hers in the semi-darkness. The breath squeezed from her lungs. She wanted him so much, she ached with it.

*Don't focus on that.*

'Where are we going?' she managed instead.

'You'll see. It's a surprise.' He threaded his fingers through hers. She stared at their linked hands. She ought to pull hers free...but she didn't.

They drove over Westminster Bridge and through Southwark. She'd assumed they were heading to his apartment. She straightened as the cab wended its way down to the Thames river-front.

Jude squeezed her hand. 'This is where we get out.'

He leapt from the cab and strode round to open her door. She took his hand and stepped out. There was a gate in front of them, but not one that led to an apartment building. 'Jude, where…?'

He led her through the gate and her eyes widened. A ramp led down to the water and the most spectacular… 'Is that a canal boat?' She couldn't call it a narrow boat—there was absolutely *nothing* narrow about it.

'It was the floating Customs and Excise Office. It's been decommissioned and is now a luxury house boat.'

She pulled to a halt. 'We're going on board?'

'I've leased it for a few days.'

*He had?*

'I thought it might appeal to you.'

It did, but… 'Why?'

'Why what?'

'Why are we here rather than your apartment, which has to be nearby, or my apartment in Fulham? Or in a private room at the Dorchester?' Why had he brought her *here*?

His face settled into familiar stern lines. 'It's *later* and I don't want to be interrupted.'

'But I don't have an overnight case or—'

'Your father had the staff at the hotel pack up

your things. They've already been stowed on board.'

Her father had been party to this?

'Come and see.'

That lopsided smile could do the craziest things to a woman's pulse. She let him lead her down the ramp and onto the boat. It was two storeys of absolute luxury. Jude led her up the wooden staircase to an open-plan living room, dining room and kitchen. There was oak furniture, big, comfy sofas and bold art on the walls.

Walking across to the enormous windows, she stared at the view of Tower Bridge. 'This is bigger than my entire apartment!'

'It's something, isn't it?'

The boat rocked gently beneath her feet and she wanted to close her eyes and savour the familiar motion.

'No expense was spared restoring it. It can comfortably accommodate twelve. Sleeping quarters are on the lower deck—four bedrooms and two bathrooms. It puts *Camelot* to shame.'

Not true—she would *always* be grateful to *Camelot*.

'Would you like a cold drink, or something to eat?'

A platter of hors d'oeuvres sat on the table and drinks were chilling in a silver bucket.

'The pantry is stocked.' He started towards the

kitchen. 'So if there's something else you'd prefer...'

She couldn't stand it another moment. It was taking all her strength not to stride across and kiss him, or say something she might regret, like *I love you.*

'Jude.' She pressed her hands together. 'You said there was something you needed to ask me.'

He stilled. 'Before we get to that...' He turned and moved back. 'Was Margot the "someone" Clay referred to?'

She couldn't decipher the expression in his eyes. She shrugged and nodded.

'You knew from the first that Margot had betrayed you?'

'No.' She pointed a surprisingly steady finger at him. 'And there are two things to unpick in that sentence. The first is, of course I didn't know. I thought Clay had lied. But when Margot kept avoiding me...' She swallowed. 'It clicked into place when I returned to London last night and found we were staying in different venues.'

He didn't say anything. It made her fidget. 'I had no plans to confront her with it, but the moment she clapped eyes on me...' She winced. 'The guilt was eating her alive. It was better to get it out in the open.'

'It was brave.'

'Nonsense.' She straightened. 'And the other thing you need to understand is that Margot didn't *betray* me. She was desperately unhappy and did a stupid thing. She didn't deliberately set out to hurt me. She didn't think to herself, "what's something I can do to hurt Cleo?"' Blue eyes throbbed into hers. It took everything she had to remain where she stood rather than sway towards him.

'You meant it when you said you'd forgive her something a hundred times worse.'

Of course she'd meant it. Margot was her sister!

He leaned down until they were eye level. 'Your father refused to let you hide out at the family home?'

She huffed out a breath. Where was he going with this? 'Look, I understood his frustration and his impatience. It was a classic case of my past coming back to bite me.'

'This past you continually refer to, Cleo, was over three years ago. Since then you've turned your life around—changed jobs, been sober, been a responsible adult. Your only crime,' he added when she opened her mouth, 'was to date a few untrustworthy jerks.'

She folded her arms. 'Your point being?'

'That you harbour no resentment towards your family for not realising that earlier.'

She folded her arms harder. 'Families can fall into patterns. They came to think of me as the problem child. Don't forget, they were grieving for my mother at the time too. Dad had no idea how to help me. And he's not the kind of man who takes kindly to feeling helpless. Margot just wanted to make everything right for everyone. All of us made mistakes.'

She hitched up her chin. 'It's taken me years to see that, though.' *And a lot of therapy.* 'So, no, I don't feel resentment towards them.'

Jude widened his stance. 'So you don't want them feeling bad about how they've dealt with you in the past? You don't want Margot to keep beating herself up for kissing Clay?'

She gaped at him. How could he even think such a thing?

His face darkened. 'Then why don't you cut yourself the same slack? Why aren't you just as kind to yourself?'

That had her speechless for a moment. 'I...'

'Since I've known you, you've continually beaten yourself up and blamed yourself for putting your family through the wringer. Over the last three years, though, you've done nothing to be ashamed of. So what if you've dated a few bad eggs? We've all done that. Unlike the majority of us, though, your romantic woes were splashed in the newspapers—*not* your fault.'

She didn't know what to say.

'The things you did when you were younger were understandable.'

'It doesn't mean I condone them!'

'When are you going to forgive yourself for them?' His hands slammed onto his hips. 'The way you've forgiven the mistakes your family have made?'

She took a half-step back.

'Earlier today you said you needed to forgive yourself. *When* are you going to do that?'

Her heart hammered. He spread his hands and scowled, but she saw the exhaustion behind it and it had tears pricking her eyes.

'What if I backslide?' she whispered, blinking hard. 'I can't afford to do that. I don't want it for me or my family. Keeping a catalogue of my sins at the forefront of my mind and reminding myself of the damage I did ensures it won't happen. It keeps me on the straight and narrow.'

His face gentled. 'Oh, Cleo.' He reached out as if to touch her, but his hand fell back to his side. Her pulse jumped and jerked. 'What if that mindset is stealing your joy?'

Maybe that was a small price to pay. His eyes narrowed, as if he'd read that thought in her face. 'Do you think Margot will ever kiss another one of your boyfriends?'

'*No.*'

'Do you think your father will ever again refuse you sanctuary?' When she remained silent, he continued, 'So why can't you believe *you* won't make the same mistakes you once did?'

She moistened her lips and frowned. Actually... that was an excellent question.

'You're not an angry teenager any more, Cleo.

You now have the strategies you learned in therapy to help you cope. Isn't it time to start trusting yourself?'

Very slowly, she started to nod. The thought of treating anyone she loved the same way she'd been treating herself had her breaking out in a cold sweat. She rubbed a hand across her chest, acknowledging silently that she didn't want a life devoid of joy.

'On Thursday night you told me I didn't need someone like you in my life.'

Her gaze flew back to his. She'd walked away from him. It was the hardest thing she'd ever done. But if she was going to start trusting herself...

'When you said I didn't need someone like you in my life, I know that you meant someone lumbered with your kind of notoriety.'

He was the head of a family with a proud heritage. He was good, kind and honourable. He deserved the best.

'But in my eyes that meant I was being deprived of someone like you—a person who has the most generous heart I've ever had the privilege to meet. It meant being deprived of your kindness and your humour and your teasing—all of which lighten my load. It meant being deprived of seeing the world through your eyes—because your way of seeing it gave me a different perspective, and that helped me find my way forward.'

Tears burnt a hole in her throat.

'On Thursday night you told me what I didn't need in my life and what your family didn't need in their lives, but what you didn't tell me is what you needed in your life, Cleo.'

Tears spilled from her eyes.

'And you didn't say you didn't love me. So the question I came here to ask you today, Cleo, is… do you love me?'

She couldn't speak. Her throat was too thick and her voice had deserted her. But what she could do was nod and throw herself into his arms.

He crushed her to him as if he meant to never let her go. She sobbed incoherently into his shoulder for several long seconds. Lifting her head, she cupped his face. 'I love you, Jude—so much. You're the most amazing man I've ever met—the *best* man. You make my life better, in every way.'

'Cleo.' Her name was a groan from his lips.

'In my mixed-up way, I thought you deserved better than me. I thought I'd just cause chaos in your life and you'd had enough of that. I didn't know…'

His fingers travelled down her cheek. 'What didn't you know?'

'That you feel exactly the same way about me that I feel about you.'

His smile, when it came, was the most beautiful thing she'd ever seen. She suspected her smile was just as radiant.

'I love a good epiphany,' she whispered.

He nodded, his head lowering to hers. Their kiss had stars bursting behind her eyelids.

Lifting her in his arms, Jude lowered them to the sofa, keeping her in his lap. She rested a hand against his cheek. 'Thank you for coming back for me.'

He half-scowled and shrugged lightly. 'I couldn't not come back for you. I fell for you the moment you crashed onto my boat and held a finger to your lips as you hid behind my chair. You've had me in some kind of spell ever since.'

She grinned. 'You were so grumpy.'

'What did you expect? You'd turned my world upside down in under ten seconds flat.'

Her grin widened. 'You were so kind, though you tried to hide it.'

He shook his head, as if still befuddled. 'I went from agreeing to hide you for an hour, to agreeing to drop you further along the canal path, to letting you stay for a week...and then a fortnight.'

Her chest fizzed with so much emotion, she could hardly breathe.

'It should come as no surprise to either one of us that I can now not let you go, that I want you in my life for good—that I want a lifetime with you. You also ought to know that I asked your father for your hand in marriage.'

The edges of the room blurred.

'Not that we need his permission, but I wanted

him to know I was serious. I want you to know that too.' He cupped her face. 'You love so fearlessly. You showed me how to love fearlessly too.'

Something too exceptional to be called happiness bubbled up through her. 'I am going to be the best wife you could ever have, Jude. I'm going to make you the happiest man alive.'

He stared at her and then he grinned—*really* grinned. 'Was that a yes?'

She grinned back. 'It's most definitely a yes.'

Could a person have been any happier than she was at that moment? Hooking a hand behind his head, she drew his face down to hers. 'I love you, Jude. I love you with my whole heart. It's all yours.'

Their lips met in a kiss that was both tender and intense, fierce and loving. It was the kind of kiss that lifted her up on a wave of optimism and *joy* that didn't lower her back again—as if her world now was bigger, better…truer.

It was a kiss that she'd remember for the rest of her life…

\* \* \* \* \*